Jungle Rock

Caroline James

Disclaimer

All characters, institutions, organisations and events in this novel, other than those clearly in the public domain, are fictitious and any resemblance to any actual institution, organisation or person, living or dead, is purely coincidental.

Cover Design

Alli Smith

First Edition Published by Ramjam Publishing 2016
ISBN 978-0-9573782-3-0

A CIP catalogue record for this title is available from the British Library.

This one's for you, Cath.
The best sister and friend a girl could have.
With my love always.

CONTENTS

ACKNOWLEDGMENTS

I am ever grateful to artist, Alli Smith, for her lovely cover and illustrations. She always gets it right.

Caroline James

CHAPTER ONE

Zach Docherty tugged at the collar of his leather jacket and climbed into a waiting chauffeur-driven car. The uniformed doorman at The Wolseley touched his hat and pocketed a handsome tip as he watched the handsome young chef. Zach was a pleasure to look after, always polite and generous, unlike many of the so-called celebrities that graced the popular eating establishment.

London was heaving and, as his ride pulled away from the restaurant and joined the nose-to-tail traffic crawling along Piccadilly, Zach yawned and slumped into the seat. He was exhausted. A new series of *The Gypsy Chef* had just finished filming and after a heavy lunch with his agent, Zach was longing for a good night's sleep.

But sleep would be evasive. The news that Bob had just given him filled Zach with uncertainty and fear. Bob's proposal offered the chance of unprecedented success but there were high odds that Zach's career could take a serious tumble.

The most popular reality TV show in recent years, *Jungle Survival*, wanted Zach on the cast. Zach and eleven other celebrities would be plunged deep into the heart of the Australian jungle, where they would be left to fend for themselves until the last man standing, as voted by the public, took the ultimate jungle crown. *Jungle Survival* went out live every evening for three weeks and was watched by millions. It could project Zach into the realms of serious stardom or finish him. He thought about some of the previous contestants who were now consigned to the celebrity slag-heap, career in ruins as the perils of the jungle got the better of them. It was a recipe for emotional melt-down and, with precious egos at stake, there was the potential for things to boil over, which could plunge a popular personality into the realms of obscurity. Bob was adamant that his protégé do the show and what Bob demanded he always got. After all, hadn't Zach made 'foraging' and 'living-off-the-land' the new buzz words in the great culinary mash-up that was today's TV? He was sure to be a jungle hit! Viewers were already salivating over Zach's recipes, his book sales had rocketed and the first series of *The Gypsy Chef* had broken ratings records on cable networks and was now set for a prime-time slot.

Zach had signed the contract. In a few days he would be winging his way, first class, to Australia; the deal had been done. He stared out of the window and watched the crowds mull about the busy streets. There was a winter's bite in the air and leaves whipped along the pavements as people snuggled into scarves and gripped the collars of their coats. November was cold, the days were short and the light had gone by late afternoon. Christmas decorations lined the streets of the capital and shop windows were brightly festooned, glittering with snowy scenes. Zach was in no mood to be festive; he'd soon be sweltering in a jungle and he didn't relish the thought.

He checked his phone and saw that he had a dozen missed calls. He speed-read the numbers, hoping that there had been a call from Poppy.

But his search was in vain.

Poppy was on a plane, skimming across the skies as she headed to a food festival in Orlando with another of Bob's high-profile clients. Poppy excelled at her job and had raced through the ranks of *Hargreaves & Puddicombe Promotions*, London's leading agency representing celebrity chefs. Bob had recently promoted her to the hallowed position of agent and Zach knew that she would be leading the high life whilst she accompanied the chef on his promotional gig. Zach longed to be with Poppy again, to run his fingers through her long red hair and hold her shapely body in his arms. It seemed as though it had only been moments since they'd met. Both had been new to the world in which they now worked, Zach as raw talent at the start of his career, and Poppy a fledgling recruit in the offices that represented him. Thrown together, they'd soon fallen in love and it wasn't long before they'd become engaged.

What a fool he'd been! He'd completely buggered up the best relationship he'd ever had. Poppy had been for keeps and they should be planning their wedding instead of being estranged, thousands of miles apart. It had all gone horribly wrong. Zach closed his eyes as rain lashed against the windows of the car, streaking across the pane like the unhappy tears that welled as he remembered the devastating event that had wrecked their relationship.

He'd been heading to a remote location in Scotland. The production company for *The Gypsy Chef* had secured a bothy to film the last episode and, as Zach set off along the bumpy track leading up the steep hillside, a runner tapped on the window of his

Range Rover and asked for a lift. Thinking that she'd accidently been left behind, Zach opened the passenger door and Dolores leapt in. Suddenly, an unexpected storm burst through the valley, the heavens opened and a deluge came down, making visibility almost impossible. The rest of the crew, who'd been following in a convoy of vehicles, doubled back to the nearest pub, unable to follow as Zach disappeared in a blanket of thick blinding fog and hammering rain. He struggled to keep control as the wind buffeted the vehicle and Dolores gripped the dashboard.

"There's a building, stop!" she cried out. They'd found the bothy!

Soaked to the skin, they slammed the door of the humble little building. Zach fumbled about with kindling and logs and lit a fire in the cold dark grate. As the flames roared, he turned to Dolores and saw that she'd pulled up an old bench and produced a bottle of malt whisky from her rucksack. She poured two generous measures and they settled down to wait for the storm to abate.

Zach could barely remember what had happened then, but knew that he'd drunk far too much. He'd woken up with a monumental hangover, beside the dying embers of the fire, while Dolores, huddled into her quilted jacket, flung the door open and announced that the weather had cleared and they'd best set off to find the rest of the crew.

A week later Instagram went mad.

Compromising photos of a naked Delores, bosom bouncing as she straddled the Gypsy Chef in the glow of a roaring fire, spoke louder than any of the excuses and apologies he'd begged Poppy to believe, and within hours his fiancée had packed her bags and left. The Dolores Photos were posted on Twitter too and the red tops were bidding high. With her job as a production company runner a thing of the past, Dolores savoured every morsel of copy as the papers ran her story. She was running all the way to the bank. Zach was left reeling and wondered if there had been more than malt in his whisky. He cursed himself for being so stupid! Whatever had possessed him to drink so much that night?

He was almost home. The lights of East Dulwich lit glistening streets as the car slowed and Zach reached for his keys. He had no urge to run up the steps to his apartment, knowing that it would be dark and empty without Poppy there to greet him. The pub next door looked inviting. Cheery voices could be heard from the Cock & Bull and Zach decided that he'd have a quick pint in the company of his friend, Ben, who worked behind the bar and always made Zach welcome. He'd ask Ben's advice about *Jungle Survival*. The no-nonsense Kiwi would certainly have an opinion and, with a slightly happier heart, the gypsy chef pushed opened the door of the pub and stepped into the congenial atmosphere.

* * *

Bob Puddicombe thrust his hands deep in the pockets of his Ozwald Boateng coat and braced himself against the cold wind whipping up the length of Piccadilly. He hardly felt the chill and smiled as he glanced at his dapper reflection in the window of Fortnum & Mason. His fingers wrapped around a string of prayer beads dangling from his wrist and he murmured a soothing chant, thanking his god for the successful outcome of his meeting. His client, The Gypsy Chef, would be a hit on *Jungle Survival*.

It wasn't rocket science to marry a foraging chef with jungle conditions and then predict the outcome. The bookies would have a field day with this bet when the news hit the headlines later in the week and Bob could already envisage his client wearing the jungle crown. He smiled as he patted his Louis Vuitton messenger bag, where a signed contract was safely stored in the soft leather folds. As soon as he reached his office in Wardour Street he would arrange for a courier to deliver it to the production company. Zach would be heading to the jungle in a matter of days and the producers of the show would soon release the names of the contestants.

Bob's phone vibrated in his pocket. He ignored the persistent buzz and thought happily of the tidal wave of cash that flowed through the bank account of *Hargreaves & Puddicome Promotions*. His business was the most successful source of culinary talent in the country and with clients topping the charts in TV, publishing and product endorsements, he was a very happy man. Bob thought about Zach Docherty. Awarded Michelin stars at a very young age, the chef had made his way to London from the wilds of Westmarland in northern England and Bob had smelt incoming talent before Zach's train touched the tracks at Euston. He soon had Zach under his wing and the charismatic young chef was an instant hit, with guest appearances on culinary shows and a cookery book to promote his adventurous recipes. His good looks, inherited from his late father who was a Romany gypsy, bode well for Zach and his legion of fans adored him.

Bob's phone continued to vibrate and, stirred from his day-dream he reached into his pocket. It was a text from Poppy Dunlop to confirm that she'd arrived in Orlando. The chef and his two commis were safely checked in to their designated five-star hotel on the Disney complex. Bob smiled. Poppy was an absolute poppet and could be relied on to ensure that his company's representation at the food festival would be first class. He had no doubt that Poppy would keep this particular chef in order, unlike the chef that she'd recently been engaged to.

Sleet began to fall and Bob wished that he'd worn a hat. He wiped at his smooth bald head as he battled through the crowds in Piccadilly Circus and thought about Poppy. Bob felt concern for the two young people, single again in their mid-twenties, but considered the episode part of life's rich tapestry and immediately turned the situation into a plus. Poppy could focus on her job and not be dreaming of weddings and babies and bachelor Zach would increase his profile with the legions of female fans dreaming of bedding the celebrity chef. After all, the press had loved the recent scandal:

Bonking in the Bothy!

The headline was an unexpected bonus and, along with the production team for *The Gypsy Chef*, Bob anticipated high viewing figures when the new series aired. There was nothing the public liked more than juicy scandal and it could only bode well for Zach's appearance in the jungle.

Bob turned into Wardour Street and almost ran

to the doorway of *Hargreaves & Puddicombe Promotions* as he thought about the new endorsements he'd lined up. He tapped in a security code and, thrusting the door open, smiled. Never mind a broken engagement - it would soon be forgotten and they'd be laughing all the way to the bank when Zach took the jungle crown!

CHAPTER TWO

Three hundred miles north of London, Zach's mother Jo sat beside a roaring log fire with her friend Hattie and sipped a glass of wine.

"Do you think we should be making the old place all festive?" Hattie asked as she looked around the elegant drawing room. The hotel's guests were dining in the Rose Room some distance away and the two women were alone in the cosy warmth as a wintery wind howled beyond the thick damask curtains and wooden shutters of the gracious Georgian building.

But Jo's expression was troubled as she stared into the flames. She was thinking about her youngest son and his broken engagement. The news had upset Jo, for she was very fond of Poppy and had hoped that Zach had found his soul mate.

"I think it's too early for decorations," she replied glumly. "I'll be sick to death of seeing them by the time Christmas comes around."

"Wonder Boy had really has buggered things up this time," Hattie said, fully aware of the reason for Jo's mood. She twirled the wine in her glass, enjoying the reflection of the ruby nectar as it danced in the firelight.

"You could be more supportive," Jo replied and banged her glass on a table. "You don't seem to be taking Zach's current predicament seriously."

"There's plenty more fish in his sea, he just needs to cast a bigger line." Hattie tossed back her drink. "I'd look on it as a bonus; the press love it. He's the new chef on the TV block and you can hardly expect him to be saddled with a fiancée at this stage of his career."

"Well, personally I think it makes him look a bit of a shit." Jo frowned. "I wonder what on earth can have possessed him. Do you think that girl might have spiked his drink?"

"I think pigs might fly." Hattie picked up the wine bottle and poured the last few drops into the glass in Jo's outstretched hand. "Any man would have done the same, just a shame she decided to cash in on it." She shook the bottle. "Shall I open another one?"

While Hattie disappeared to the cellar, Jo considered Zach's situation. He was a young man about town with a lot of commitments. Since Jo had re-opened her hotel, *Boomerville*, as a retreat for guests in their later years, Zach, amongst his other jobs, worked with her chef to create menus to ensure that Jo's guests dined on the very best. It certainly helped bookings to have a celebrity name above the restaurant doors and, as his popularity grew, so did their takings. People flocked from all over Westmarland to sample Zach's recommended dishes in the splendour of the Lake District setting. But as much as Jo wanted success for her son, she worried that the celebrity status he'd created might one day backfire, and episodes like his experience in the bothy ultimately affect his future happiness.

"Get yer gob round this and let's see you crack a smile," Hattie's broad voice boomed out. She was busy tugging the cork out of a dusty bottle of Merlot. "I found this in the cellar; it's so old it must need drinking."

Jo watched Hattie open the wine.

There was nothing Hattie liked more than a good laugh and a chin wag but Jo thought that she was making the most of Zach's latest escapade. She knew that Hattie loved Zach; he was, after all, her godson. But Hattie had different views on parenting and Jo found it difficult to leave Zach to fight his own battles. Jo thought about her shenanigans with Hattie over the years and the many relationships that hadn't always run smoothly. Zach's escapades were mild in comparison. Jo could write a book! She watched Hattie settle her ample body into a comfy chair and smiled. With Hattie as general manager at the hotel, the years had flown and they'd enjoyed happy times that would keep the memory bank stocked for the days when they were no longer able. Running the business had never felt like work with Hattie alongside, in fact Jo was sure that working together kept them both young. Combined with a good dose of gossip they thrived and The Dolores Photos had certainly provided that.

"I wonder what Jimmy would think," Jo said.

"His big brother wouldn't dwell, what's done is done," Hattie said. Jimmy, Jo's eldest, ran a bar in Barbados and had his own set of complications to deal with on a nightly basis.

"I suppose you're right," Jo said. "Jimmy would laugh it off." She felt mellow from the wine. "I just hope Zach behaves himself; he has a new series coming out soon."

"I think we can safely say that whatever dilemma the lad might find himself in, with his looks and charm and the money he's paying Bob to mind him, he'll come out on top."

"Yes, you're right - Bob always knows what's

best."

"Aye, good old Bob, all beads, bangles and Buddha." Hattie glanced at Jo and saw that she was smiling. "Should we get the decorations out?"

"I suppose so." Jo thought about the tired old fairy that Hattie insisted on placing at the top of the Christmas tree each year and her faded garlands in the shape of dancing elves which had seen much better days.

The two friends turned to each other and raised their glasses.

"Here's to Christmas!"

* * *

Four and a half thousand miles west of Marland, Poppy sat in her hotel room and studied an itinerary. The thick envelope, marked *Miss Poppy Dunlop*, contained several sheets of instructions from her American festival co-ordinator. They were neatly typed onto letter-headed paper and embossed with a smiling Mickey Mouse. The Epcot Food Festival was in full swing and Poppy had busy days ahead ensuring the chef she had under her wing lived up to expectations.

She glanced out of the open window. A hot sticky breeze wafted the muslin drapes, ribbon-like, into the room. Christmas trees lined the walkway surrounding a leisure area and she could see Mikey and Minnie Mouse characters, amusing little ones in a children's park. Poppy didn't feel in the least like Christmas and couldn't imagine enjoying the festivities so far away from home.

She searched for her chef amongst the happy

families and found him beyond a low white picket fence, sitting on a lounger by the pool. Poppy could almost feel the sweat on the brow of their star attraction as he tilted a cooling beer and guzzled thirstily. His beautiful ebony skin glowed under the hot sunlight and muscles rippled on his torso as he caught the attention of the bikini-clad girls relaxing by the pool. Poppy hoped that she wasn't going to have her hands full keeping the chef to his tight schedule, which consisted of a series of TV interviews, an exclusive luncheon and several demonstrations to a ticketed audience. His stay would culminate in a grand finale with attending celebrity chefs from Europe, serving their signature dishes to a VIP guest list of foodie attendees from all over America. Chef would be aided by two commis chef side-kicks, who worked at his restaurant in London and were in awe of his celebrity status. Poppy could see the commis as they splashed about in the pool. Their pale mottled skin appeared to be frying in the hot sun, turning red on thin angular bodies unused to being so exposed, far away from the demands of Chef's Michelin-starred restaurant.

Poppy fancied a swim too. She felt hot and tired after their journey, but she knew she needed to distance herself from Chef and certainly not parade about in a swimsuit. They'd had a very close encounter on the plane when she'd accidently knocked his arm and spilt his after-dinner drink. Baileys and ice was not a good look when soaked into the crotch of his Versace jeans and she'd made it much worse by dabbing at the area with her napkin. Horrified that Chef's instant erection was about to burst through the fabric, Poppy had dashed to the restroom where she'd splashed cold water on her burning cheeks and tried to compose herself. The wink that he gave her when she returned to her seat suggested that she might have more that his cooking skills to worry about during the trip.

Poppy decided that she'd forgo a swim and take a shower instead.

As she stepped into the walk-in shower, warm jets hit her body and she reached for the perfumed shower gel from a bottle decorated with a smiling Mickey Mouse. Poppy thought of Zach. So many times he'd led her into their shower and caressed her body before making love under the pulsating spray. Poppy ached for the man that she'd been engaged to; he was the love of her life and she doubted that she'd ever get over him. She remembered his mop of black wavy hair and his beautiful tanned body and groaned in an agony of frustration. Zach's brilliant blue eyes had made her knees buckle every time he glanced in her direction.

Poppy had been hopelessly in love but she'd been completely humiliated and the thought of him in the arms of another, with incriminating photos splashed all over the press, was more than she could bear. She turned the jets to freezing. The icy spray made her gasp and, pulling herself together, she endured the cold shower for a few moments, getting all thoughts of Zach out of her mind as she watched the foamy water drain away. Grabbing a thick cotton towel, logoed with the Disney insignia, she wrapped it tightly around herself and padded across the room until she reached the mini-bar, where she poured a glass of chilled water from a bottle labelled with a smiling Micky Mouse.

These wretched mice get everywhere! Poppy thought angrily. She lay down on the king-sized bed. She needed a power-nap before preparing Chef for his first event.

As Poppy closed her eyes, she tried not to let Zach back into her thoughts. She had a job to do and she must do it well. Her own career was the only future that mattered now!

CHAPTER THREE

Zach opened one eye and peered at the clock beside his bed, groaning when he realised that he'd overslept. Lifting his head from the pillow, he attempted to swing his legs to one side but the room seemed to be spinning and he fell back on the bed.

"G'day!" a voice rang out. Ben burst through the bedroom door and in moments had opened the blinds.

"Jeez..." Zach groaned again, stuffing the pillow over his head as brilliant sunshine cut through his vision like a knife.

"There's a car on its way with your name on it," Ben said and leaned over to shake Zach. "You betta grab your gear and get moving." Ben pulled the duvet from Zach's inert body but Zach tugged it back and rolled over, enveloping himself in the folds.

"Mate, your boss has been on the blower and you need to get in the office." Ben wrenched hard and Zach fell onto the floor.

Startled by the impact, Zach sat up. His head throbbed and his throat felt razor raw. "I'm never going to drink again," he mumbled as he staggered to his feet. "Please tell me I'm not all over the papers."

"Nah, I steered you clear of trouble." Ben walked into the bathroom and turned the shower on. "Get yerself scrubbed up, Bob wants you suited and booted and ready to rock, you've a flight to catch in the morning." Ben was used to taking calls from Bob when the agent couldn't get hold of his client. He frog-marched Zach into the shower and, when he was sure that Zach wasn't going to drown himself, headed to the kitchen to make some strong coffee.

Ben looked around the kitchen and shook his head; his friend seemed to have gone to pieces since Poppy left. The once immaculate and homely apartment was now a shambles, with clothes strewn over the furniture and remnants of half-eaten meals congealing on a variety of plates and take-away boxes. Ben sighed. This was the umpteenth time he'd bought Zach home from the pub and put him to bed. The chef seemed to be drowning his sorrows since he'd split from Poppy and at this rate would soon be completely submerged. It was a good thing that the new gig had come about and Ben hoped that a stint in the Australian jungle would have Zach back on the straight and narrow. There wasn't a chance that he could booze himself up when he had to do weird tasks to get food and survive and, with any luck, Zach would get his head straight and come back a better man.

"Told your ma yet?" Ben asked.

Zach appeared with a towel wrapped around his slim waist. He yawned as he stepped over the debris to take the mug of freshly-brewed coffee that Ben held out.

"Oh man, that's a life-saver." Zach slid onto a stool opposite Ben. "No," he said, "and I'm not sure that Mum's going to be too thrilled about it."

"Best get it over then." Ben pushed Zach's mobile across the counter.

"I'll tell her later."

"Like when you're about to board your flight?"

"I haven't got time now."

Zach tried to recall his conversation with his agent. Bob had told him that the production company would provide all the kit needed in the jungle and a recent holiday in Peru ensured that Zach's immunisations were up to date, but there was a list as long as his arm in the office that needed checking before he began his trip.

"Got some decent clobber to take too?" Ben frowned as he looked at the piles of soiled shirts and jeans. Zach clearly hadn't been near a washing machine in weeks.

"I'll do some shopping today." Zach slid off the stool and stretched. The injection of caffeine had worked wonders and, as it shot through his veins, he felt his head clear and realised that he could be away for some time. "Do you think you could get someone in?" He cocked his head towards the mess.

"Yeah, yeah, I'll suss it out." Ben knew that his cleaning lady at the pub would be more than willing to have a root through the celebrity chef's personal space. "It'll be sparkling as much as the jungle crown I expect you to bring back with you."

Zach shuddered. The thought of the jungle and the fact that he was about to take part in a competition under the glare of reality TV was sobering. He needed to speak to Bob and get a clear brief on how to deal with everything. Thank goodness his agent was accompanying him on the trip.

"Guess I'll catch you when I get back." Zach looked wistfully at his friend then thrust out his hand. "Thanks for looking out for me."

"Shot bro!"

The two men touched knuckles then hugged.

"You'll be awesome." Ben smiled and, with a cheeky grin and a wave, disappeared out of the apartment.

"I really hope so," Zach whispered.

The apartment bell rang. A car had arrived to take Zach to the office and, with a sigh, he went to get dressed.

* * *

Poppy stood beside the stage in the darkened auditorium and watched her client. Chef was regaling the audience with highlights from his career as he skilfully filleted a piece of fish and juggled pans on a hob.

He could certainly entertain.

The audience were applauding and one or two let out a *Whoop!* as Chef flamed his dish in brandy with a theatrical twist of his arm. The female presenter was leaning in to ask questions as the star turn of the day put the final touches to a three course meal and presented his dishes with a flourish. The audience roared their appreciation and stood to applaud.

The presenter was concluding the session, informing all gathered that they were about to enjoy the menu that Chef had demonstrated, during which time he would be walking around the tables to answer any questions.

Poppy hurried over to speak to Chef as the

Disney hospitality team swung into action and served lunch.

"You were brilliant!" She watched him pack up his knifes and place them in a secure box. The commis chefs hovered, wiping down every inch of the demonstration area, loving the attention they were getting.

"I know." Chef grinned and leaned in to give Poppy a kiss on the cheek. "What do I have to do now?"

"Just be nice, chat and socialise and then finish up with a book signing."

Poppy watched him remove his bibbed apron and smooth the elegant lines of his white tailored jacket. He held the apron out and a commis swooped in.

"Can we get a drink after this?" Chef's hand hovered over Poppy's pert bottom and she twisted away. She was getting used to manoeuvring herself out of close encounters of the chef kind and had spent the last twenty-four hours doing precisely that.

Disney hospitality far exceeded anything that Poppy's party had imagined. The previous day had been free for them all to explore the theme parks. After an early call, they'd been greeted by a VIP host in the hotel foyer. A limousine whisked them to the parks where their host took them to the front of the queues, by-passing long lines of holiday-makers. Poppy became a child again and for a few brief hours was lost in the make-believe world of The Magic Kingdom. Chef sat close, snaking an arm around her at every opportunity.

Poppy watched Chef work the tables and weave his own particular magic over the paying guests. It never ceased to amaze her that chefs had become such icons and made cooking such a sexy affair and her thoughts soon turned to Zach. She'd been surprised to hear from the office that Zach was about to fly to Australia to appear in *Jungle Survival.* Whatever had possessed him? Poppy wondered who the other contestants would be and frowned as she imagined a string of shapely models and actresses, eager to bare all. But perhaps that was why Zach was going. She thought angrily of The Dolores Photos and bit down on her lip as a rush of tears burned at the corner of her eyes.

An arm slipped around her waist and lips gently brushed her ear. "Something upset you?" Chef whispered. "I can make it all better."

"No, not at all." Poppy pushed his arm away. "It must be the air-con. I have an allergy." She side-stepped his huge frame. "If we're all done here, we can make a move."

Grabbing her clip-board and holding it like a shield, Poppy gathered her party and eased them out of the auditorium. There were times when she felt that no amount of money could pay for the pressure she was put under, and with a glare in Chef's direction, she guided them to their next appointment.

* * *

"He's doing *what?*" Hattie said. She had a mouthful of shortbread and a mug of coffee in her hand and stopped in her tracks as she watched Jo stare at her mobile phone.

"Zach's going into the jungle. He's a contestant on *Jungle Survival.*"

"Oh my." Hattie smiled and wiped a spray of crumbs off her chest.

"He's at the airport with Bob; they're about to board a plane."

"Well I never." Hattie put her mug on the desk and stared at her friend. "How do you feel about that?"

"Astonished."

"It might do him good."

"Or not."

"Fancy a bracer?"

"Start pouring."

Cradling mugs of coffee, laced with a good slug of brandy, Jo and Hattie sat in the conservatory and looked out at the garden beyond.

"It doesn't seem five minutes since he was a little boy running all over this lawn with his brother," Jo said as she stared thoughtfully across the neatly manicured grass.

"And now he's running off to Australia."

In the distance, a group of guests appeared from the meadow, where a clairvoyance course was being run in an old gypsy caravan. Originally horse-drawn, the caravan had been John's pride and joy, brightly painted with little wooden steps. It was a perfect setting for an intimate group. Boomerville hosted many courses for residents to enjoy and it was Jo's hope that a stay at the hotel would inspire middle-aged boomers and set them up with new and inspiring skills to use in their later years.

"Another successful event," Hattie said as she watched the beatific expressions of the participants as they drifted down the garden, confident that the spirits of their dead granny and Rover, the family pet, were beside them, whispering and woofing encouraging words from beyond.

"I wish I could see into Zach's future," Jo replied. "I hope he's not making a terrible mistake."

"Well, if he is, he's picked the right place to make it. That show's watched by millions. Perhaps we should run something similar here?" Hattie closed her eyes and began to plan out a jungle camp, set in the meadow. "The old 'uns would love it! Prancing about like Bear Grylls, cooking over an open fire, sleeping under the stars. It has 'winner' all over it."

"It has mass suicide all over it," Jo replied. "Hyperthermia and food poisoning."

"Think of the low overheads. We could bring Wonder Boy in to teach them how to skin a rabbit or two, a bit of camp-fire bonhomie and all that stuff."

"Hattie, will you please be serious. My son is currently on his way to the other side of the world, where he'll be exposed to any amount of danger; he's emotionally vulnerable and I'm worried about him."

Hattie sat up and opened her eyes.

"Oh, get a grip," she said. "Can you imagine what he's getting paid for this stint? How can he possibly go wrong? They'll have him stripped down to his six-pack before the opening credits have run. He won't even need to open his mouth and the phone lines will be pulsating as fast as every female viewer's heart. Your Zach has made his finest career move yet." Hattie reached for Jo's empty mug. "Get that grumpy expression off yer face and let's send him good luck wishes for his arrival in Aus." She stood and glanced at the group in the garden. "Perhaps we can get that lot to send him a mystical sign..."

As Jo watched Hattie walk away, she felt cross.

She knew that Hattie was probably right but Jo had a niggling feeling that Zach's trip wasn't going to run as smoothly or as successfully as everyone expected. A mother had an instinct about her offspring, but in this case, Jo hoped that her instincts would be proved wrong.

CHAPTER FOUR

Zach jumped into a courtesy car and, as he waited for the vehicle to pull away, he watched the frantic activity at the entrance of the filming location. The production team were moving props and pushing huge storage containers across the site. Everyone was busy and intent on their jobs as they called to one another, yelling instructions. He was eager to find out what would be happening next and, having undergone and passed a thorough examination at the medical centre with Mac the Medic, the on-site doctor for the duration, Zach knew that his jungle adventure was about to begin.

They began to move and as the car coasted along a wide and dusty road, leaving the town of Willyumbah behind, Zach took in his surroundings. He gazed across the banks of Billabong Creek and watched it wind through the lush countryside. Dressed in boots, combat trousers and a multi-pocketed shirt, Zach was ready for the jungle, but he couldn't rid himself of a gnawing fear in the pit of his stomach. As he watched the creek, glistening like a snake as it flowed over rocks and poured through deep gorges, he felt nervous.

It was early and the morning sun was rising

above the rich green caldera, reflecting shafts of brilliant light across the extinct volcanic crater, the area carpeted with farmland and rainforest. Zach had spent three comfortable nights at the Hilltop Hotel, a lovely residence that overlooked the creek, set in landscaped gardens in the middle of a grazing farm. Zach had wandered and swum each day before settling down to some much needed sleep. Accompanied by Bob, their journey to Brisbane had seemed to last forever and throughout the twenty-three hour flight, Zach had been restless. Whilst Bob hurried to do some shopping in duty-free in Dubai during their stop-over, Zach sat in a café. He had no one to buy gifts for and couldn't bear to torture himself by viewing beautiful jewellery that would look wonderful on Poppy's porcelain skin.

All of the contestants were housed in separate hotels before they met up in the jungle. This ensured that no one knew each other beforehand and they had time to adapt to the time difference before filming began. Bob and Zach's hosts at the Hilltop Hotel were thrilled to have a reality show contestant on their guest list. Gary and Simon, who owned the property, fussed around the two new arrivals, much to the delight of Bob, who relished the over-the-top attention and sat drinking prosecco with his new friends long into the night.

As the sun rose through the morning mist and the tip of Mount Wumbah appeared, silhouetted in the valley surrounding Hilltop Hotel, Zach had said goodbye to Bob. Bob would be travelling separately to stay in accommodation provided for family and friends.

"Just be you, dear boy," Bob said as he walked

across the veranda and stared at the awe-inspiring sight. "I know that you'll make us all very proud." He turned and Zach could see that his agent had a tear in his eye.

"I'll probably be back in a week or less," Zach said. He knew he hadn't a hope in hell of lasting to the end of the contest, no matter how badly Bob wanted him to, and his heart felt heavy. Was this another moment in his life when he'd let someone down?

"Nonsense!" Bob said. He could see Gary and Simon running across the grass and gave them both a little wave.

"Hello there!" Simon called.

"There's a delivery for Zach!" Gary said.

The two men raced up the steps and thrust out a package.

"I wonder who can have sent it," Bob said. "Hurry up and open it, your car's waiting."

Zach ripped through the packaging and, as he peered into the box, he grinned. A slab of confectionary lay on a bed of tissue. "It's Marland Mint Cake," he said. "Explorers take it on expeditions."

"Sir Edmund Hillary ate mint cake while climbing Mount Everest." Simon stared at the parcel.

"It's made of glucose and peppermint, my favourite," Gary said.

"What does the card say?" asked Bob.

Zach retrieved a small envelope and tore it open. *"Get yer laughing gear around this lot and stop feeling sorry for yerself! Me & yer mam will be glued!"* He smiled. *"Love and kisses from the old 'uns."* He broke the bar into pieces and handed them out. "It's from my Aunty Hattie."

"Magnificent Marland." Bob licked the sweet treat. "Home of our Gypsy Chef!"

The car had begun to slow and Zach saw that they'd left the main road to bounce across a track. Eventually they came to a clearing where a small team from the production company waited beside a helicopter.

Shit! Zach thought. *They're going to drop me out of that thing!*

A woman moved forward to greet Zach and he realised that a camera was filming. He grabbed his rucksack and pressed his Cattleman hat firmly onto his head, then, taking a very deep breath, forced his most appealing smile.

"G'day!" Ava, a popular Australian TV host, rushed forward to shake Zach's outstretched hand.

"Hi," Zach said.

"It's the Gypsy Chef!" Ava announced. "Welcome to Jungle Survival!"

* * *

Bob stretched out in a comfortable cushioned cabana and looked around at the well-heeled guests enjoying an afternoon beside the pool. The Willyumbah Palazzo was probably the most luxurious hotel Bob had ever stayed in and he was determined to enjoy every moment.

Not for Bob the accommodation provided by the production company. He had adamantly refused to stay in the mediocre Willyumbah Motel, where families and friends of the contestants were being put up until their loved ones exited the jungle and they were reunited in splendour at the Palazzo, under the full glare of the TV cameras. Bob was familiar with production budgets and he'd upgraded himself before they'd boarded the flight. After all, it wasn't as though he couldn't afford the extortionate hotel tariff and it would all go down on expenses. Since the break-up with his partner, Anthony, it had been nothing but work for Bob and he felt he deserved a bit of luxury. Marriage hadn't been all it was cracked up to be and no matter how many prayers and chants Bob uttered, his soul needed some serious soothing. He still reeled from the pain of discovering that Anthony had been unfaithful, having thought their relationship was for keeps. But as Bob sipped ice-cold water and looked around, he determined not to think of Anthony for the next few weeks.

Bob stroked the soft cotton layer covering the padded recliner and thought about Jo. Zach's mother would have loved to stay in such luxurious surroundings and it was a shame that neither Jo nor Hattie could get away. But Boomerville was busy in the run up to Christmas and they needed to be at the helm of Jo's business. Bob had become close to Jo in the time that he'd worked with Zach and he valued her friendship. They'd spent many an evening cosied up over a bottle of wine, as Jo shared memories of John, Zach's father, and Bob had been fascinated to hear all about the handsome gypsy who had stolen Jo's heart. Having made a success of his life, John had settled into family life with Jo but he never forgot his Romany heritage and had taught Zach and his brother, Jimmy, all the skills of foraging and living off the land. Bob was grateful to the enterprising man, for he'd blessed Zach with a talent that would prove fruitful for them all.

The pool stretched endlessly and Bob toyed with the idea of sliding off his bed and into the inviting water. It would do no harm to get some sun while he was away; after all, London was dismal at this time of year and he'd make quite an attractive splash with his tan in the home-coming photos. He wondered what Zach was up to. Rumour had it that the celebrities were already making their way into camp by one route or another. No doubt some would travel down the creek by boat but others may be dropped by air. Bob yawned. He had no doubt that Zach would handle whatever was thrown at him.

Bob closed his eyes and muttered a few soothing chants. *"Au, Nama Shiva..."* he repeated several times and let the words send him into a semi trance-like state.

"Hi there!"

Drops of water sprinkled across Bob's body and, startled, he sat up. Gary and Simon had glided to a halt at the foot of Bob's cabana and both gave jaunty waves as they splashed about. Clad in miniscule matching speedos, their bronzed skin and golden hair gleamed.

"Fancy a cocktail?" Gary said. "There's a poolside bar and you don't even need to get out of the water."

"We know the barman too!"

Bob smiled at this welcome intrusion and, reaching for his sunglasses, wriggled down the bed and slid into the water.

"Race you!" Gary said and broke into a breaststroke while Simon shot ahead with a crawl. As Bob sedately swam across the glorious lagoon he silently thanked his god for bringing him to the jungle and, with all thoughts of Zach forgotten, joined his new friends.

* * *

"Come on Jo, it's started!"

Hattie had arranged a sofa in prime position in front of the large screen in Jo's lounge and sat on the edge as she waited for *Jungle Survival* to begin. The opening credits had rolled and the presenter was gibbering on about the new series and the celebrities entering the jungle.

"Bleedin' hell, she's thin." Hattie studied the screen. "What's with the drop-crotch jeans?" Hattie held her head to one side and studied Ava's outfit. "She looks ridiculous."

Jo dashed into the room and flung herself on the sofa. "Be quiet!" she said and sat forward. "They're about to announce a contestant."

The camera switched to an aerial shot and a helicopter came into view. On board, another camera was fixed on the pale and terrified face of Zach, as he sat on the edge of the open-doorway and stared with horror at the view beneath.

"Oh, my gawd!" Hattie covered her face with her fingers. "He'll die before he's even got there!"

Jo had her eyes closed and she gripped Hattie's arm. They listed to the shrill voice of Ava as she explained that Zach was attached to an experienced parachutist who wouldn't begin their descent until Zach gave the word.

"Jump!" They all yelled, chorusing from Marland and mid-air. Jo and Hattie opened their eyes and watched with horror as Zach leapt from a chilling height.

"He hates heights," Jo whispered as they watched Zach's face fill with fear. "He wouldn't even sit on a stool when he was little."

As Zach fell at terrifying speed they held their breath. A remote camera attached to his helmet recorded his contorted expression and rapid de scent. Suddenly a parachute opened and Zach seemed to bounce before slowing to a glide. His eyes were wide and tear-stained as he gazed around and, realising that he was safe, began to hoot with joy as they came to a gentle landing on the soft brown earth below.

"Did you enjoy that?" Ava said as Zach scrambled to his feet. An instructor reached over to unhook Zach from his flying kit.

"I want to do it again!" Zach cried and he grabbed the host in a bear hug.

"Blimey!" Hattie said.

"Thank God." Jo sank back into the sofa.

They watched Zach begin to make his way on foot into camp and, as the camera panned away and an advert break began, both let out a sigh.

"I need a stiff one." Hattie stood and poured out two large brandies. "We've got three weeks of this, I'm not sure I can stand the tension."

"That's if he makes it to the final." Jo took a drink from Hattie's outstretched hand and took a large gulp.

"Oh he will," Hattie said. "Old Wonder Boy will sail through the tasks and the public will love him." She sat back on the sofa. "Just you wait and see."

* * *

Poppy was putting the finishing touches to a thank you speech that Chef would use later that evening. She paused and searched through her notes, determined to ensure that she hadn't forgotten anyone from the Disney Corporation. It wouldn't do to leave out any of the festival's hosting dignitaries.

Things were going well. Chef had so far performed superbly at all the events and tonight he would be demonstrating to leading Disney chefs and their kitchen teams. He would showcase his fine-dining skills and justify why he was the proud holder of three Michelin stars at his much acclaimed restaurant in London's West End, where foodies and critics from all over the globe came to sample his eclectic cuisine.

Poppy was secretly terrified of being anywhere near the Disney chefs.

They'd been summoned that morning to the kitchens of the Chief Executive Chef, where Chef and his commis were given a briefing about the grand finale event. As Poppy stood in the vast building, which reminded her of an aircraft hangar, and while Chef asked questions, she'd nervously glanced around as she made notes. It felt as though she were on a culinary battlefield, as teams of uniformed chefs swung into action to prepare for the massive scale catering in this part of the festival park. With military precision, orders were issued and cries of "Yes Chef!" yelled back. The kitchen was a blur of silver equipment and white-coated bodies dashing about with furious haste around gigantic pots and pans. The commis chefs were enthralled and hung off every instruction being uttered, their eyes and mouths wide open.

"Did you get all that?" Chef asked as they were escorted out of the kitchen and driven back to their hotel. His hand trailed lazily over Poppy's knee.

"Yes." She knocked his hand away. "Do you know exactly what you're doing for the finale?"

It was a pointless question; Poppy knew that Chef would have memorised every word of instruction from his Disney colleagues. It was more than his reputation was worth to screw it up and, as the VIP guests would be voting on the dishes, she was aware that Chef intended to take victory over his rivals and revel in all the accompanying publicity.

"Come and have a nightcap with me after tonight's demo?" Chef asked as their car pulled into the driveway of the hotel.

Poppy stared through the windows at the perfectly manicured grass and white picket edging, set against splendid colonial style buildings and a brilliant blue sky. She wondered if she'd accidently stepped onto the set of The Truman Show.

"One little drink won't hurt." Chef edged closer and Poppy could smell the musk of his expensive aftershave and felt heat radiating from his delicious skin.

"I'll be too tired, I need to stay fresh."

'But you like dating chefs," he whispered. "And I've got more stars than your ex."

Poppy swung round and glared at Chef. How dare this arrogant, egotistical man think that she was dating, groupie-like, the rising stars of the celebrity chef world! Zach had two Michelin stars and didn't need the addition of another to put him in the same league as Chef. After all, Zach had a successful TV series and was currently in *Jungle Survival.* She was about to retort but suddenly stopped. Why was she defending Zach? It wasn't as if they were an item any more.

"Ah, I touched a nerve." Chef smiled and held out his hand. The car had stopped and a doorman, dressed in white flannels and a blazer edged in gold, ran forward to open the door.

Poppy ignored Chef's hand, thanked the doorman and strode purposely ahead.

"I'll see you at six thirty," she called over her shoulder to Chef and his commis. "Don't be late!"

Her notes were perfect and the speech all done. Chef would get another standing ovation from his audience that evening and Poppy knew that it was no more than he deserved, for he carried out his duties with the art of a pro. His cooking skills were unquestionable but it was Chef's ability to entertain an audience that put him into the super-chef league and ultimately gave him earnings far beyond those made behind a kitchen stove.

Poppy looked out through her window, where a Florida sunset was creating magic over Mickey and his friends in the gardens below. The red-orange glow, combined with pretty Christmas lanterns strung around the trees, made Poppy feel mellow and she wondered why she was refusing Chef's advances and behaving like Miss-High-and-Mighty. Would it do any harm to have a drink with him? He was stunningly attractive, charming and kind, and to her knowledge had no hidden agenda that she need be worried about.

He simply wanted to get laid and Poppy was his dish of the day.

What would it matter if she had a quick tumble? She couldn't argue that business and pleasure didn't mix, look at her relationship with Zach. No one would know if she spent the night with Chef. The commis were on another planet, lost in the world of the Disney culinary machine and no doubt planning their next career moves.

She wandered over to the closet and as she opened the mirrored door, let her hand trail along the clothes hanging on a rail. She reached for an olive-green sheath dress and held it to her body and, as she studied her reflection, she remembered the last time she'd worn it.

It had been the night of her engagement to Zach.

Poppy had been determined to throw the dress away but somehow it had made its way into her case. The colour matched her eyes and the silky softness clung to her curves and Poppy remembered the way Zach had gazed at his new fiancée, as if trapped by a powerful spell.

Not long after that night, the spell had been broken and now Poppy angrily threw the dress onto the bed. She heard the clock in the garden chime six times and realised that she'd be late if she didn't hurry. But as she turned to step into the bathroom, she looked back at the dress.

Maybe it was time to put a few ghosts to rest.

CHAPTER FIVE

Life in starter camp was tough, as Zach and the celebrities got to know each other and shared frugal living quarters. They spent much of their time wondering which of those amongst them would be able to do the daunting challenges.

With only rice and beans as their staple diet, the contestants were tasked with a trial each day and, after competing against each other, the winner would be moved to Happy Valley, the ultimate home camp for the group when they all got together again. Happy Valley was paradise in comparison to the starter camp and everyone made it their aim to get there as quickly as possible. Food was more readily available and the facilities included shelter from the sudden rain that whipped up and soaked them at unexpected times during the day and night.

So far, Zach hadn't really entered into the spirit of the jungle.

Realising that there were contestants amongst them who would struggle to go without food and live on basic rations, he'd made little effort in any of the tasks.

"Why are you letting these daft girls win so they can fill their faces in Happy Valley?" Lenny Crispin asked as he poked at the fire with a long stick and ran a chubby hand across his face.

"There are others who need some decent grub," Zach replied and glanced over to the sleeping form of a middle-aged man who was snoring loudly. "Rod's already getting weak without any meat and vegetables."

Lenny stood up and stretched. "I've put a lot of work into getting this," he said and patted the tight-fitting vest hugging his belly, "and I don't intend to lose it."

Zach watched the portly figure as Lenny moved away and began to chat to a well-endowed woman, lounging in a hammock. He wondered what Lenny's motives were? For his jungle stint laid bare his past misdemeanours and the viewing public were fully aware that Lenny was a con-man, who had pretended to be a celebrity chef, and embezzled thousands when he attempted to set up a cookery school in Ireland. But the public seemed to love Lenny and his quaint mannerisms and Zach could remember the headlines when Lenny was sent to prison: *Ready, Steady, Crook!* With his cockney charm and gift of the gab, Lenny was known as a come-back-kid and now worked as a presenter on a day-time show investigating fraud, a subject he excelled in. He'd jumped at the chance to be in *Jungle Survival.*

Zach picked up the stick that Lenny had abandoned and, adding more wood to the fire, poked it into place.

"Keep the 'ome fires burnin'," a voice called out and Zach smiled as he saw that Rod was awake.

Rod Zephr, an ageing popstar, had been an icon in his day. With his bleached quiff and long straggly hair sticking out above a ravaged body, Rod had lived life to the full on tour with his band in the drink and drug-filled days of the seventies and eighties.

"Is there anything cooking in that pot?" Rod asked and swung his bony legs over the side of a camp bed.

"Just hot water, I'm afraid. Can I make you a cuppa?"

"Anything me old mate, me belly's rumblin'." Rod had never lost his northern accent and fans felt that it was part of his charm when he growled out the lyrics of popular hits, whilst gyrating on stage during his 'Legend' tour.

Zach began to prepare tea and as he poured boiling water onto the leaves, he thought about life in the camp. After they'd all made their way into the jungle, it hadn't taken long for everyone to settle in to their new environment. Camp was sparse, with make-shift beds and hammocks laid out around an open fire; they only had logs, rocks and the jungle floor to sit on. One of the girls had been upset the first night, having broken a nail getting out of a canoe as she paddled slowly up the creek to camp. She'd sobbed into her sleeping bag then complained of an allergy to rice and beans and everyone agreed that she needed to win the next day's task and move swiftly onto Happy Valley. After a meagre breakfast, the task, to run through a pool infested with fish guts, began. Allowing her to surge ahead, the other contestants dropped liked flies and insisted that they couldn't go on. Lenny, who was starving, wasn't playing the game and ran a close second, but the allergy-ridden celebrity romped her way to the other side after she'd tripped Lenny, face-down, in the swamp. When pronounced the winner she set off, happily anticipating a nail file and some decent tucker on her arrival in Happy Valley.

The cameras filmed silently in the background and recorded every move that the contestants made and Zach and his fellow campmates soon forgot that they were being watched. They thought that they were deep in the jungle, far away from the massive production unit. But in reality, the crew were very close to the celebrities and had to move around quietly so as not to be heard. There was a restricted road to the site, from where Ava broadcast the shows. Accessible only by four-wheel drive, the studio was connected to the camps by a large suspension bridge that hung across the valley. To the viewing public, the camp appeared to be open to the elements, but Happy Valley was, in fact, largely covered by tarpaulin layered with hessian, high above the probing eye of the camera lens. Every moment of the contestants' day was filmed then edited in a way that made the scenes more watchable. Trials were performed some distance away and participants had to walk through pathways in the jungle to get there.

Close to the camps was a small lagoon with a waterfall.

This provided bathing facilities and contestants could also wash their clothes. Scenes were filmed of pummelling, rinsing and wringing by celebrity hands that had never been near a box of soap powder and were unused to such chores. More interesting waterfall action involved panning in on a bikini-clad body as glamour model, Cleo Petra, seductively lathered her ample breasts, held pert and upright in a tiny string halter, thus ensuring that her designer swimwear collection was flying off the shelves back home.

"Wouldn't mind crash landing face down in them," Lenny said as he watched Cleo saunter back into camp. "Better than any airbag..."

The celebrities were hungry. With only four of them left to face the next trial, Zach felt concern for Rod. Lenny and Cleo were holding up well on their diet of rice and beans but Rod seemed to lack energy and Zach was determined that the old rocker be next over the suspension bridge to receive a decent meal in Happy Valley. As they gathered to hear what Ava had in store, Zach wondered what the viewing public thought about his own pathetic attempts to win the tasks.

The Gypsy Chef, known for foraging and living off the land, had turned into a wimp. Zach knew that he was losing weight through lack of food and his lethargy towards winning anything would surely mean that he'd soon be voted off the show. But right now his concern was for others and he needed to make sure that Rod was on his way to decent meal.

Zach focussed on what the host was saying.

"So guys, find a box and we'll begin." Ava swept her arm in the direction of four upright Perspex boxes, which were open from above.

Zach nodded at Rod and gave him a reassuring wink, then climbed into a box.

"You've got ten minutes, after that its sudden death and only two of you will go through." Ava smiled. "And you may have company! Remember guys, if you want to get out you just have to raise your hand and we'll have Mac the Med get you right outta there."

Zach looked around. Lenny was laughing and seemed slightly hysterical while Cleo sat forward to ease her cleavage into position. Rod had his eyes tightly closed. Zach wondered how many minutes his fellow contestants could endure.

"Are you ready?" Ava said. "Let's go!"

* * *

"Would you believe it?" Hattie was aghast. "He's only bleedin' raised his hand before the first grub has even landed!" She sat with Jo and stared in horror as Mac the Medic led Zach out of his Perspex box. "Even that lass who's full of silicone has lasted longer!"

"I think Zach's doing it on purpose." Jo's eyes were glued to the screen.

"Well, he's making a right tit of himself if you ask me," Hattie said. "Calls himself the Gypsy Chef?" She folded her arms and shook her head. "He hasn't won one trial yet."

"Oh dear, look at Lenny." Jo winced as she watched the rotund little con-man splutter and stagger away from his box. His hair was full of slime and meal worms. "He didn't last long."

"You've got to hand it to old Cleopatra, she'd made of stern stuff." Hattie studied the model who seemed determined to battle it out. Slime, fish guts and what seemed like thousands of wriggling grubs oozed over Cleo's chest.

Ava counted the clock down and as it struck time, she announced that both Rod and Cleo had won and would be leaving camp to join the others at Happy Valley, where a hearty meal awaited them.

"He'll be on the next plane home." Hattie was cross. She watched Zach and Lenny walk out of shot as they made their way back to camp, heads downcast at the prospect of another hungry night ahead.

"They'll both be in Happy Valley soon, I'm sure it's not as bad as it seems," Jo replied. She frowned as she watched her beloved son. He seemed to be losing weight and Jo felt sure that his hips hadn't stuck our quite so much when he'd arrived in the jungle.

"Or his hotel," Hattie said. "Once they start voting, the public will want to see a hero not a has-been."

"I think you need to give him a chance," Jo said, but in truth she wondered if Hattie was right. The Gypsy Chef had yet to prove himself, and even though Jo felt sure that Zach had deliberately held back on the tasks to send others through, she doubted that the public would see it that way.

"Well, all this worrying has made me thirsty," Hattie said. "Fancy a snake bite?" She headed over to a glass-fronted cupboard where Jo kept a range of liqueurs.

"Let's hope he has a better day tomorrow." Jo studied the strange-looking concoction Hattie held out.

"To Wonder Boy!" Hattie said and, raising her glass, downed her drink. "Let's hope he succeeds in his jungle journey!"

* * *

Bob sat in the family and friend's viewing room and studied the large screen. He watched Zach's every move and he noted that the boy had lost a little weight. It accentuated his six-pack and, combined with the wonderful tan that was developing, made his client the eye-candy of the show. Zach had the shadow of a beard on his chiselled face and Bob thought that it added to the young man's rugged appeal.

Bob wasn't in the least concerned that Zach was losing the tasks. He knew that the chef was playing a blinder. Selfless, he was putting others first so that they could benefit from the additional food that was available, leaving only meagre rations for himself. The public would lap it up! But the current jewel in the jungle was the excerpt being shown on screen as Lenny searched through a mound of dung for a key to allow him into Happy Valley, little knowing that Zach had held back to let him win. The dung monster, covered in unmentionable matter, looked ecstatic as he waved goodbye to Zach and set off to join the others and have his first decent meal in days. As the camera closed in on Zach sitting alone in camp with only a small bowl of rice and beans to eat, Bob could almost hear a collective sigh of pity from the home nation.

The credits rolled and everyone began to make a move to their hotels. One or two people smiled as Bob strutted past, while others looked away. The contest was fiercely competitive, possibly more so with the family and friends who were determined to see their own loved one battle through to the end and lift the jungle crown.

Bob jumped into a vehicle and instructed the driver to take him to the Willyumbah Palazzo. He'd booked a table for dinner that evening on the roof-top terrace and was looking forward to enjoying the alfresco setting in the company of Gary and Simon, who were coming over to join him. The two men, who'd both worked in the hospitality industry all over the world, were very good company. Bob had lots in common with his new friends and was anticipating the evening with pleasure.

All in all, things were turning out rather well!

CHAPTER SIX

Poppy lay on a massage table and felt a pair of experienced hands knead and pummel the taught skin on her back. It was warm in the dimly-lit, vanilla-scented room and the only sound came from the haunting notes of Peruvian pan pipes, playing softly in the background.

Poppy closed her eyes and let the motion and music wash over her. As her mind drifted, she visualised a beach with swaying palms. In the distance a man strolled towards her, his strong muscled body stark against the soft golden sand and Poppy smiled as she ran towards his outstretched arms and fell into his loving embrace. But as she turned to gaze into his brilliant blue eyes, she gasped.

The man in her dreams was Zach.

"Is everything alright for you, ma'am?" the masseuse asked.

Poppy sat up. It was impossible to relax, the dream was so real. She longed to be with Zach, meandering on the make-believe beach, not lying on a bed a zillion miles away hoping another's hands would cure the pain of her loss.

"Yes, that was great, thank you." She reached for a robe and thrust her arms into the thick cotton fabric and waited while the masseuse left the room, leaving her client to dress.

Poppy slipped into a pair of jeans and a comfortable t-shirt and ran her fingers through her tousled hair. She felt a shiver tingle down her spine as she remembered the previous evening when Chef had reached out to stroke her tumbling locks. Now, in the cold light of day, she wasn't sure if the shiver was anticipation or fear.

Chef's demonstration had been a huge success and he'd run over the allocated time as the Disney chefs and their teams, alongside executives from the corporation, enjoyed his entertaining performance. He'd produced a stunning selection of fine-dining food, which they'd all been invited to sample, whilst giving a running commentary on what it took to be at the top of one's game in the culinary world in Europe. As Chef walked Poppy back to their hotel, his buoyant mood was infectious and, to celebrate, she willingly agreed to have a drink with him. The night was balmy and they sat in an open-air bar overlooking a marina, complete with an old-fashioned river boat. Poppy could hear the faint sounds of a jazz band as the steam powered paddle-wheels propelled a dinner cruise through the dark waters.

When Chef slid his arm over her shoulders, she didn't resist. And when he suggested a nightcap in his room, Poppy found herself holding his hand as they made their way through thickly-carpeted corridors.

Chef dimmed the lamps and went to the mini-bar where he took out a bottle of champagne and popped the cork with ease. "You look beautiful," he said. "That dress really suits you." He handed her a glass, then turned. "Would you like some sounds?"

Poppy nodded. She sipped her drink and let the bubbles explode on her tongue; it was delicious! She watched as Chef flicked through the digital channels on the TV. He reached out and pulled her to his side and, as he searched for a music station, his ran his free hand up and down her spine, softly caressing her skin, which tingled beneath the sheath dress. Poppy placed her glass down. She longed for Chef to rip the dress off her body and throw her to the bed. It had been ages since she'd felt so aroused and casting her inhibitions to the gentle breeze that came through the open window, she turned and found the fastener at the nape of her neck, then began to slip the dress off her shoulders.

"And he's coming out!"

Poppy spun round.

Chef had paused in his search and began to laugh as Poppy stared at the screen in horror. Trust Disney to have every world-wide station available on their network! Zach was being removed from a Perspex box and looked miserable as he faced the camera and mumbled something unintelligible about disliking creepy crawlies.

"The Gypsy Chef," Chef said. "What a wimp." He shook his head and flicked past the channel until he found some late-night music. "Good job you ditched him, babe." Chef pulled Poppy into his arms. "What you need is a real man." He began to kiss her neck and run his hands all over her body, his fingers edging the dress up her long legs.

The image of Zach had shocked Poppy, he looked so alone and lost. Clearly out of his comfort zone, his shoulders were slumped as he walked out of camera shot and Poppy was sure that he'd lost weight.

"Relax," Chef whispered as he tried to nudge her tense body towards the bed, but Poppy had come to her senses, with all feelings of passion gone. Pushing his arms away, she grabbed her bag and rushed to the door where she fumbled about until the lock gave and released her into the corridor.

"Poppy!"

She could hear Chef calling and, afraid that he might come after her, she began to hurry towards the elevator. The doors flung open and both commis chefs fell out. Much the worse for wear, they giggled when they saw Poppy.

"Join us for a drink." The young men slurred their words as they staggered back to the elevator.

"Go to bed," Poppy said sternly, "you've got a long day tomorrow." Brushing past their unsteady bodies, she flung herself forward. The doors closed and as the elevator cruised to her floor, Poppy stared at her reflection in the tinted mirror panels. Her face was white.

"Disney Survival!" Poppy whispered. "Get me out of here!"

* * *

Boomerville was busy. Every bedroom was taken and the restaurant had bookings for weeks ahead. *Jungle Survival* was generating new business from far and wide with guests wishing to sample menus created by the Gypsy Chef. Visitors from further afield wanted to see the building that had been his boyhood home.

"We should do tours," Hattie said as she watched a group of young girls followed by a party of pensioners wander down the hallway on their way to afternoon tea.

"We're running out of cookery books," Jo replied as she sat in reception with Hattie. She stroked the glossy cover of the book at the top of a stack of volumes, where Zach's face beamed behind a variety of edible foliage. *Foraging for Friends with the Gypsy Chef* had become a best-seller since Zach's TV appearances.

"Good job we got Wonder Boy to sign so many," Hattie said. "I stuck another fiver on the cover price."

"Do you think he's alright?" Jo asked anxiously and ran her finger around the outline of Zach's handsome face.

"You're still worried that he's being cast in a bad light?"

"Well, he hasn't won any tasks yet and looks quiet and very moody."

"Just wait for tonight," Hattie said. "He's joining up with everyone in Happy Valley, the contestants will go crazy. Do you think we should bring your wide-screen down and set it up in the lounge? We could charge for seats."

"No, I don't think so." Jo shook her head. She didn't want the guests to witness her misery if Zach found he wasn't welcome in the home camp. After all, the celebrities were in there to win tasks not fail them.

"Oh, get that haunted look off your face, before the wind changes," Hattie said. "He's done it on purpose; he always was a bit soft, wanting to feed and pamper people. He's let the weakest get through." She yawned. "From now on it'll be down to business."

"I hope you're right."

"Do you think we should get the kitchen to liven the food up a bit while *Jungle Survival* is on the telly?" Hattie picked up a leather-bound folder and flicked through the restaurant menu. "We could have a nice set menu; snake soup, kangaroo roast and a spider soufflé." She glanced sideways at Jo, who was shaking her head and looking at Hattie as though she'd lost the plot.

"Only joking." Hattie grinned and leapt to her feet. "I'm off to make meself look beautiful for the onslaught tonight; the restaurant is full from seven. I think I'll have a nosey round the cellar too and get the porter to get the Christmas decorations out."

"If you must."

"Why don't you give Bob a call and get the jungle news from the coal-face? Let him reassure you that Wonder Boy's doing OK."

"That's a good idea." Jo looked more cheerful. She reached for her phone and searched for Bob's number.

"I'll catch you later." Hattie leaned forward. "See you on the sofa!" And giving Jo a peck on the cheek, she turned and went to work.

* * *

"Sweetie," Bob said, "do you *know* what time it is?"

Jo pressed the phone to her ear; she thought she heard muffled voices and wondered if she'd caught Bob at a bad time.

"Sweetie, can you hear me? It's three-thirty in the morning!"

"Oh, I'm sorry. I've been trying you for a couple of hours and forgot that you're nine hours ahead. Is this a bad time?"

"Well, no darling, but it could be better." Bob sighed. "Is it something important?"

Jo was sure she could hear voices getting louder

and someone was giggling in the background. Perhaps it was a crossed line?

"If you're anxious about Zach, you probably know as much as I do...oooh..." Bob's voice raised a notch then faded away.

"Should I call back tomorrow?"

"Perhaps be a better connection then." Bob sounded breathless. "Don't worry about our boy, watch the show tonight. Gotta go, sweetie, love yoooo..." Bob's voice faded away and the line disconnected.

Jo sighed; she knew she really shouldn't bother Bob with her worries.

She stood on the driveway at the front of the hotel and tucked her mobile into a pocket then turned to peer through the windows. Guests had gathered in the lounges to enjoy a pre-dinner drink and Jo could see Hattie in the throng. She wore a smart black dress and as she distributed menus and took orders, she smiled at everyone and seemed to radiate joy. The perfect host, Jo thought to herself as she watched her friend. Hattie may have a broad accent and be a true Marland girl, but she had been popular from the moment Jo had opened her doors to the public, in what felt like a lifetime ago. A great deal of water had passed under the bridge since those early, heady days, when it was sink or swim with the business and Hattie had turned up on the doorstep. A young divorcee with children to feed, she was desperate for a job. Her circumstances mirrored Jo's own, for Hattie had also been left by a philandering husband, and had a family to bring up and a living to make. They'd had many ups and downs over the years and life had thrown a few curve balls, but the latest one had unsettled Jo, for it involved one of her own precious sons and she would fight like a tiger to protect him. Thank goodness she had Hattie to keep her on track. Hattie always had a cheerful word and no matter how tough the going got, she always found a positive spin.

Jo shivered, she was getting cold. As she walked across the gravel, something caught her eye and she looked up. Strung across the entrance was a garland of tired-looking elves and pinned to the middle a notice read,

"Home of the Gypsy Chef. Happy Christmas!"

* * *

Bob placed the phone in its cradle and threw himself on the bed. Did Jo not have a clock in Marland? He sighed and closed his eyes and tried to visualise her as she anxiously waited for the evening's episode of *Jungle Survival.*

She'd be dressed in some divine little ensemble that complemented her figure, for she was still lovely in middle age. Jo had turned many a head in her time and Bob could understand why. With her bright copper hair, always cut in a jaunty style, and twinkling eyes, she was lovely arm candy for any man.

Bob smiled as he thought about some of Jo's dalliances whilst he'd known her. She'd landed in hot water on more than one occasion but in Bob's book, Jo could do no wrong. Hattie gave Jo a good run for her money too and Bob sighed fondly as he remembered Hattie's Caribbean lover. Mattie and Hattie had been the talk of Marland for weeks and Bob hoped that Hattie managed to fly to Barbados for a sun-filled frolic whenever the fancy took her.

"Anyone there?" Voices called out from the Juliet balcony, where the glass sliding doors were open to the humid night. Bob looked up. In the distance the glittering lights of the gold coast reflected across the darkened lagoon. It was an enticing sight.

He gathered himself.

"We're coming to get yoooo!"

All in a day's work! Bob smiled.

CHAPTER SEVEN

Zach bent down and piled as many logs as he could carry into his arms. As he stood, he felt his muscles tighten under the weight. Tasked with keeping the camp fire going day and night, Zach had also been voted camp cook and he found that he was suddenly enjoying his time in the jungle.

No longer having to hold back on trials to enable the weaker to get through, Zach was longing to get in on the action and prove himself. But the public were keen to see those less able endure the perils, in order to win food for the celebrities. A female popstar seemed to be the target of the nightly votes and she absolutely refused to participate. No kangaroo testicles passed her plump lips, nor would she lie in a trench and be covered in rats and, unable to win any food, the camp mates were very hungry.

"Let's hope Lady Muck strikes gold this morning," Lenny said as he fell into step behind Zach on the path back to camp. A member of the aristocracy had been summoned to set out with Rod on a secret mission. "I'm so bleedin' hungry I could eat one of these logs." Lenny held a log in each hand and sweated profusely as he lumbered along.

"There's bound to be food up for grabs," Zach replied as he thought about poor Rod, paired with the most obnoxious camp member.

"I soddin' hope so." Lenny panted as he tried to keep up. "Rod will do his best and Mrs Crunch and Gravel might surprise us."

They'd reached Happy Valley and Zach began to lay the logs neatly around the fire as Lenny placed his offerings straight onto the blaze.

"I'm going to have a shower," Zach said and grabbed his towel. "You coming?"

Lenny was climbing into his hammock and was focused on swinging his pudgy leg in an attempt to hoist his weight. Finally, he had a hold and, with a grunt and an exhausted sigh, collapsed into the moving canvas. "You go ahead, mate, I'll keep an eye on everything here." Within moments, Lenny was sound asleep and loud snores echoed through the tranquillity.

Zach set off. He whistled as he walked to the waterfall and gazed at the lush vegetation and shafts of sunlight streaking through the trees.

"You sound happy," Cleo said. She was sitting on the edge of the lagoon, wearing a tiny white bikini and she smiled as Zach approached.

"It's a beautiful day," Zach said. He placed his towel on a rock and stripped down.

"Ever considered modelling?" Cleo studied Zach's naked body. Her eyes wandered over every muscle and came to rest on the bulging contents of Zach's tight briefs. "I've a swimwear range that you'd look good in." She raised her eyebrows and smiled.

"I'll stick with being a chef." Zach plunged into the pool and splashed about in the shallow waters.

"Come and scrub my back for me," Cleo said and slid off the rock. She glided across the water until she reached the waterfall then slowly stood and turned her back. "Come on, I won't bite."

She held a bar of soap in a perfectly manicured hand and beckoned Zach with one elegant finger. Mesmerised, he moved across the pool. As he took the soap, Cleo turned and purred seductively,

"Nice and hard," she whispered, lifting her long silky locks off her toned, bronzed shoulders. 'Mmm, that's just how I like it!"

* * *

Poppy was apoplectic! She could hardly bear to look at the screen. It had taken her ages to find the channel and as she sat on the edge of her bed and watched the scene unfolding before her, she wanted to scream.

Was Zach really so gullible? Couldn't he see that the glamour model was teasing him, anything to get her enormous breasts and miniscule bikini in front of the camera? Worst of all, Zach seemed to be lapping it up! He was making it his mission to ensure that Cleo-bloody-Petra was getting the best soaping down she'd ever had and every crack and crevice must surely, by now, be squeaky clean!

Poppy flicked the TV off and flung the remote to one side then watched it slide off the bed and spin across polished tiles. She felt like kicking it and took a deep breath to compose herself. No doubt Zach would now be tumbling in a hammock with Cleo, for the show she'd watched was a re-run. It hadn't taken Zach long to get over his broken engagement! Poppy gritted her teeth and closed her eyes as she remembered Zach's pleas for forgiveness when The Dolores Photos were made public. Thank goodness she hadn't listened to him.

A knock on the door made her jump and she ran to answer it. Chef stood in the doorway with his commis chefs either side.

"You're late."

"Oh crikey, I'm sorry, I forgot the time."

"This is the most important gig of the festival."

"I know. I'll be right with you."

"We'll wait in the foyer, hurry up!"

Chef turned on his heel and marched down the corridor. The commis gave Poppy a sympathetic look as they ran behind.

Poppy slammed the door and sighed. *Damn you Zach Docherty!* If she hadn't been watching his pathetic appearance in the jungle she would have been downstairs, ahead of Chef, punctual and prepared for the evening ahead. She glanced in the mirror. *Get a grip Poppy!* she admonished herself as she applied a coat of lipstick and pushed a comb through her hair, and then, grabbing piles of paperwork and shoving them into her bag, Poppy ran out of the room to face Chef and the grand finale.

* * *

"By gum, the water in that lagoon will be at boiling point." Hattie chuckled. "One highly profitable swimwear contract safely in the bag!" She wore a grin as wide as the screen as she watched Zach cavort with Cleo.

"She seems like a very nice girl," Jo said and frowned as Zach turned and Cleo soaped his back.

"Aye, perfect daughter-in-law material, the masses in Marland will love her." Hattie sat upright and leaned in towards the screen. "Oh, we're getting a full frontal!" She laughed when she saw that Zach had a bulge in his briefs and a camera had zoomed into his crotch. He quickly dipped into the water.

Hattie wiped tears from her cheeks and shook her head as the camera panned back to Happy Valley in time to catch Lenny falling out of his hammock. He was still asleep as he rolled to the ground.

"Comedy gold." Hattie tucked a tissue in her sleeve.

The camera panned to a group of contestants who were milling around a small wooden chest. The aristocrat and male pop star had won the challenge and were proudly displaying their spoils.

"They've got food," Jo said excitedly. "Rabbits and vegetables, Zach will be pleased."

"Yep, Wonder Boy needs to get back and get cooking, never mind frolicking about in that pool, and the sooner his does his own trial the better."

Jo's face fell. "Do you think the public will vote against him?" she asked anxiously and thought of The Dolores Photos and now these scenes with a glamour model. Zach did seem to be a bit of a cad.

"Who knows," Hattie replied. "You'll have to ask Bob where he thinks his protégé is in the popularity stakes. Right now, I haven't a clue."

The credits rolled and Jo stood and turned the TV off. "Are you staying here tonight?" she asked. Hattie lived in Marland, where she had a lovely home on one of the more mature roads in the town. It overlooked the fells and hills that surrounded the area. When she was working, Hattie often stayed in a guest room in Jo's house, which joined the hotel.

"Aye, I am. I'll be up in a bit. I've a few things to do."

"Will you lock up?" Jo yawned as she headed for the stairs.

"Leave it with me."

Hattie waved as Jo disappeared, then stirred herself and went through a door, hidden in a wall panel, and into the hotel. Most of the guests had already gone to bed and Hattie knew that many had formed jungle parties and got together in each other's rooms to watch the show. No doubt there were lots of shenanigans taking place behind closed doors and Hattie smiled as she began her rounds. She felt that she should capitalise on the fact that Zach had grown up at Kirkton House, or Boomerville, as it was called today. She was working on an idea that could prove lucrative. There was no harm in adding a few extra pounds to the coffers for their ultimate retirement fund and Hattie was sure that Jo, if she knew, would have no objection.

Lifting a large bunch of keys from a hook in reception, Hattie began to patrol through the rooms. She looked around the elegant hotel that felt like home to so many and decided that they needed to add more Christmas decorations over the coming days. As she locked the front door and turned off the lights, she smiled. It was great to see the old place alive and kicking again, just the way Hattie intended it to stay!

* * *

Bob was eating his lunch. The canteen that was laid on for friends and family also supplied food for the crew and Bob wasn't impressed with the choice. He watched the queue tucking into stodge and calorie-loaded dishes and was glad that he'd stuck with a salad and lightly grilled chicken and looked forward to a meal at his hotel that evening.

Everyone had been gathered early that morning. It was the first day of the evictions and the unfortunate celebrity who was voted out first by the public would be greeted by his or her loved one.

There was tension as people gathered around a screen to hear Ava make an announcement. Bob wasn't in the least worried that his client would be tripping over the jungle carpet. After the feast Zach had produced last night, Bob was confident that the chef was staying put. The contestants had marvelled at the dinner they'd received and their stomachs were groaning with appreciation as they all settled down for the night. What one could do with rabbit and a few vegetables!

He looked up at the screen.

"G'day!" Ava said as she stood in camp, surrounded by celebrities holding hands. Everyone looked anxious. "As you know, I'm here to announce which celebrity has been voted by the public to do the next trial and also to announce which of you will be leaving the jungle today."

There followed a drawn-out process as contestants were told, "It's not you," and a cheer went up when Zach was announced as the next celebrity to do a trial.

Thank God! Bob thought. He smiled. Chief cook and fireman would now prove his worth by bringing home a full deck of meals for camp and Bob was confident that there wasn't a trial in the world that would defeat Zach.

A cry rang out and everyone spun away from the screen to see that a woman had burst into tears and collapsed, sobbing uncontrollably. The crew summoned Mac the Medic who, with assistance, escorted the casualty from the room. She was the mother of the newly evicted popstar, distraught that her daughter's future earnings had taken a sudden nosedive.

Bob gathered his belongings. No point in lingering with this lot. He was heading over to Hilltop where Gary and Simon were preparing a lunchtime soiree for a group of their friends. Everyone wanted to meet Bob and hear about his client, and he was looking forward to a day in the country. He threw his messenger bag over his shoulder, picked up a bottle of water and went in search of a car.

CHAPTER EIGHT

The grand finale of the Epcot Food Festival was the closing event of what had been a memorable week for Poppy and her chefs. Now, as they stood by their work stations in a vast banqueting hall, Poppy felt her nerves take hold. The event they had been building up to was about to begin.

In a few moments time, the doors would open and five hundred guests would flood in. The VIP diners had paid a staggering amount of money to get the golden tickets, which would entitle them to sample taster portions of the signature dishes of forty of Europe's finest chefs. Everyone would vote for their favourite dish and at the end of the evening, the winning chef would be announced. It was an accolade that every chef wanted to display on his restaurant wall.

Poppy glanced at Chef and his team and saw that they were busy with the final touches. Renowned for his global cuisine, Chef would prepare a ragout of brill with autumn truffle and bacon foam served on lemon oil. They'd been working all day in the Disney kitchen in preparation for the evening and as Poppy mentally counted the empty plates, stacked high on Chef's station, she hoped and prayed that he would be up to the task and fill the plates swiftly with the winning dish. Her role was to meet, greet and guide guests to her client. Armed with information about Chef, from his London restaurant to his cookery books and the many ranges of culinary paraphernalia that he endorsed, Poppy had her work cut out.

Suddenly, the bright lights overhead were dimmed and thousands of fairy lights twinkled from swathes of dark fabric lining the ceilings and walls. A Disney executive stepped forward and spoke into a mic.

"Good evening, ladies and gentlemen, please welcome - the Cirque du Soleil!"

Acrobats magically appeared, spinning into the room, and a host of circus performers glided and spun through the air across silver wires lacing the enchanting scene. Poppy was entranced. The colours were dazzling as dancers whirled into position around the hall.

"Chefs, are you ready?"

A hearty chorus shouted back, "Yes!"

"Let battle begin! Please welcome your guests."

The executive stood back and the doors at the end of the hall slid open to reveal five hundred expectant faces. They cheered as they witnessed the magnificent sight ahead of them. Forty food stations awaited, with tantalising tastes, wine-laden tables and entertainment of the highest standard from the world's leading troupe.

The guests surged forward.

The next two hours flew by in a flurry of activity as Chef and his team skilfully produced five hundred portions of food. Poppy had no need to worry about guests coming to Chef's table; the branding she'd organised and the delicious smell and appetising food was a stand-out enticement and crowds flocked around. Poppy found that she had to constantly move people on to ensure that everyone got a plate, as the commis chefs cooked like whirling dervishes, sautéing and serving the food. Like a mechanical production line, they produced plate after plate and Chef continued to beam his trademark smile. He was gracious with his guests and eased through the session like a pro, his three Michelin stars worn with pride and determination, confident that no one would beat him.

Suddenly the room stilled.

Acrobats, high on a trapeze, slid down a silky rope and dancers gracefully came to a stop.

"Ladies and gentlemen." The executive looked out at the expectant crowd and let the tension build. "We have a result!"

Poppy stood next to Chef and realised that she had taken his hand. The commis chefs laced their arms around the little group and Chef winked at them all. He stood tall and proud and made ready to move forward.

"Oh my, this is a wonderful result." The executive shook his head. "It seems that the voting has been staggeringly close and the winner has won by the smallest margin."

Poppy felt Chef squeeze her hand as the commis pressed his back and thrust him forward.

"And the winner is..." There was a loud drum roll. "Pascal Aussinon!"

A thunderous round of applause rippled through the hall and a French chef stepped forward to take the award. Cheers and hoots bellowed from the appreciative crowd as people rushed to pat Pascal on the back.

Chef was rigid. Poppy could feel the tension in his body and, taking a deep breath, she silently counted to ten then said, "Can I get everyone a drink?" She turned to the commis who looked pale and exhausted. They nodded in unison. "I'll be right back," Poppy said and leaving her group, she jostled her way through the throng to the bar.

As Poppy waited patiently to be served, she looked up and saw an acrobat with a sad clown's face. He was climbing a ladder and making ready to jump off a trapeze. She reached for a glass of wine and stared at the clown.

Their eyes met.

Poppy raised her glass and gulped back the much needed drink, and, placing the empty glass on the bar, she whispered to the clown, "Hang on! I'm coming with you!"

CHAPTER NINE

Jo wandered through the reception rooms and admired the decorations that were gradually appearing throughout the hotel. Somewhere, beneath a pile of dusty boxes, she knew that she would find Hattie, supervising the annual activity. The trees in the front rooms were dressed with red and gold ornaments, and fir cones, laced into tartan ribbon, made pretty garlands on the stairs. Pictures were framed by holly, with its bright red berries, and fairy lights were strung around the entrance hall.

"By heck we've had these a good many years." Hattie emerged and admired her work. She had dust smeared across her cheeks and tinsel in her hair as she reached out to turn the lights on. Jo crossed her fingers and prayed that Hattie wasn't about to blow herself up. The lights slowly flickered into life.

"Crackin'!" Hattie said. "They live to light another year. Now come this way, I've got a surprise for you." She led Jo through the front door and held up her arms. "Look!"

A four-foot garden gnome stood at the entrance. Jo remembered the gnome from Hattie's garden in Marland. Hattie had dressed him in a tired Santa suit and grubby white beard and as she clapped her hands, the gnome began to dance.

"He's on a remote, his nose will light up in a

minute," Hattie shouted above the Christmas melody. "What do you think?"

Jo thought that Hattie had lost her mind but knew that it wasn't the right moment to dampen her enthusiasm.

"Lovely," she said and she stared at the flashing gnome.

A brisk wind whipped across the drive and Jo rubbed her hands together and blew warmth onto her fingers. December had blown in with a northern chill and there was talk of snow on the forecast. Jo beckoned Hattie away from the dancing gnome and closed the door.

"Brrr," Hattie said. "He'll freeze his balls off out there."

"Do garden gnomes have balls?"

"Of course they do," Hattie said. "He's now a Christmas gnome with silver glittery ones."

They walked down the hallway into the cocktail bar where a cosy fire burned in an iron grate. Hattie stood close to warm her legs. "Fancy a snorter?" she asked.

"I don't see why not." Jo went to the bar to find a bottle of wine and poured them both a glass. She joined Hattie by the fire and they settled into comfy chairs.

"The end of his jungle stint," Hattie said and held her glass up to the fire. "Here's to our boy, let's hope he makes it." She took a sip of her drink and stared at the flames. "He's done a great job keeping that camp fire going and feeding them all."

"I don't know how he managed it, with all those trials as well." Jo stared into the fire too and thought about Zach's tribulations.

"I thought he was a gonna when he got stuck in that

underwater cave." Hattie's eyes misted over.

"I knew he'd come through with the eating trial," Jo said. "God knows how he managed to chew through a kangaroo penis."

"He's had worse in his mouth."

"I wish he wasn't spending so much time with that glamour model."

"Are you mad? It's far better than hanging round with Lenny who farts and belches and whines about his rapidly decreasing belly all day."

"He seems to have made a friend in Rod; they get on very well."

"Aye, the old bugger has quite a twinkle in his eye." Hattie grinned. "I wouldn't mind rocking around Rod's Christmas tree. Do you think we might have the coming home party up here?"

As the days passed in the jungle, the public had voted for Zach to do most of the trials and Jo and Hattie speculated long after each episode was shown, wondering if viewers loved or hated the Gypsy Chef. Jo had spoken to Bob on several occasions and he'd told Jo to stay calm. It was in the jungle bag, so to speak. Bob had every confidence that Zach would be triumphant and the press and media were simply whipping up intrigue by suggesting that there was anything between Zach and Cleo.

"We'd better get ready for dinner," Hattie said and edged her body forward. "Ouch!" She suddenly winced and fell back into the chair.

"Are you alright?" Jo sat up.

"Aye, just a bit of heartburn, shouldn't drink red wine at my age."

"Can I get you something?"

"Nope, I'm fine. I'm going to get ready, before the

guests come down."

"If you're sure," Jo said and watched Hattie head for the kitchen, no doubt intent on sampling the evening's menu, heartburn or not.

Zach would soon complete his time in the jungle and then be heading home. Jo wondered if she ought to go and meet him at the airport; with no girlfriend waiting for him it might be rather nice to have a familiar face in the arrivals hall. Perhaps Hattie would like to go too?

Jo decided that she would discuss it with her later and, finishing her drink, picked up their glasses and went to get changed for the evening ahead.

* * *

Poppy was back on home turf and couldn't believe how good it felt to be wandering through the cold and blustery streets of East Dulwich, far away from the perfect world of Disney. The last couple of days had been exhausting and with an after-show party that seemed to go on all night, she'd been too tired to get any sleep on the long flight home.

They'd all arrived back to a freezing cold UK. As the party prepared to go their separate ways at the airport, the commis chefs collected the mountain of luggage from the carousel and piled it onto trolleys. Poppy was keen to find a taxi and head home and, after thanking the chefs and taking her trolley, she turned to Chef.

"I'll be compiling your press pack over the next couple of days and will be giving a very good feedback report to Bob; you were excellent and everyone loved you." Poppy gritted her teeth and pasted a bright smile on her face. "I'll send you a copy as soon as I've finished it."

"Don't bother," Chef said.

"But you were wonderful, you were runner-up to Pascal, it's a fabulous achievement out of so many highly acclaimed chefs."

"I don't do 'runner-up'." Chef leaned in close. Poppy felt his warm breath brush against her cheek. "And I don't like girls who play games."

Poppy wanted to whip her knee up and give Chef a wake-up call in his nether region but instead she smiled sweetly and said that she'd soon be in touch. She'd spent most of the after-show party fighting off his advances and as Chef, sullen in defeat, was obnoxiously drunk, she'd had to steer him away from anyone who might be offended by his behaviour. It was with some relief that she got the commis to help her escort Chef away from the party and back to his room, where he fell into a deep and drunken sleep. Thank god they were home and his Disney mission accomplished.

Poppy turned towards the Cock & Bull and decided that she'd go and say hello to Ben. It was ages since she'd seen her good friend and she'd bought him a gift from Orlando. Poppy had known Ben throughout the time that she'd been with Zach and the Kiwi had been a shoulder to cry on when everything went wrong. She pushed the door open and made her way through the bar. The pub, a hangout for trendy professionals, was buzzing.

"Watcha beautiful!" Ben leaned over the bar and gave Poppy a kiss. "Don't you look mint."

"I've got you a present," Poppy said and she pulled a package from her bag.

"Hardout!" Ben thrust his hand into the brightly coloured bag and retrieved a Mickey Mouse doll. "Just what I always wanted, so cool," he said.

"You can throw it in the bin if you like," Poppy said. "I've seen more of Mickey Mouse than is humanely reasonable."

"Good trip?"

"It was a great trip but crazy company."

"That's chefs for you."

"You can say that again."

"Can I get you a glass of Pinot Grigio?"

"Yes please, make it a large one."

Poppy settled on a stool and took a sip of her drink. Ben moved to and fro to take care of his customers and when he got a break, he returned.

"Have you been watching the jungle?"

"I've tried to avoid it." Poppy glanced at her watch and made a mental note to get back to her digs before the show started. She was staying with a friend who would no doubt be glued to *Jungle Survival* too.

"He's still in there." Ben polished a glass. "It's hard to say which way the public will vote."

"Oh, they'll keep him to the end," Poppy said. "Everyone's clamouring for him to get cosy with Cleo in her hammock; it's only a matter of time."

"I thought you weren't watching?" Ben raised an eyebrow.

"Oh, what do you think?" She gave a half-hearted smile and took a sip of her drink. "Of course I'm watching; it's compulsive viewing."

"It's the final tomorrow, shall we watch it together?" Ben asked. "Zach is a hero round here with the locals and I've had to stop the cleaning lady cutting up his clothes and selling bits off. I'll get a big screen in;

there's sure to be a crowd."

"If you must." Poppy finished her drink and hopped off the stool. "I have to go."

"See you tomorrow. Thanks for Mickey."

Ben flashed Poppy a smile. He grabbed Mickey Mouse and placed him in prime position on the bar. "What a waste!" Ben shook his head as he watched her walk out of the pub.

* * *

Life was quieter in camp as contestants were eliminated and, with the competition drawing to a close, only four celebrities were left. Zach, Lenny, Rod and Cleo sat around the fire eating breakfast and contemplated their last evening together; they all knew that the winner would soon be announced.

"There's bound to be another trial and it's gonna be the hardest," Lenny said. Despite getting through to the final, he wasn't looking forward to being put to the test yet again, having failed miserably at everything he'd attempted.

"I think we'll get a slap-up meal and booze if we complete it." Cleo arched her back, and smoothed a tiny vest top over her enormous chest.

"Well, I'm up for the challenge; the jungle has made a new man of me." Rod sucked in his stomach and flexed the muscles in his arms. "What do you think, Zach?"

"Like a racing snake." Zach smiled. He'd become very fond of his camp mates over the last few days. All had their strange idiosyncrasies but were fundamentally decent people. Even Lenny, who had driven everyone mad with his moaning, had mannerisms that charmed and Zach thought that now that Lenny was going straight and had turned away from crime, he would make a fortune. Despite the fact that Lenny had pretended to be a celebrity chef years ago, in the jungle they'd discovered that he couldn't so much as boil an egg. Cleo seemed to want constant reassurance and at times bottled her feelings and isolated herself but she was very sweet and they all felt the need to protect her. Rod, on the other hand, was an open book. When the camp had been tired and hungry, he entertained with tales of life on the rock star road and soon had everyone laughing. Rod rounded off each day with a camp-fire sing-song medley of his famous hits and they'd all joined in. Amazed that he'd reached the final, Zach wondered how his own image looked to the outside world. In the day-to-day boredom of it all, it wasn't difficult to be yourself in the jungle and he'd forgotten that the cameras were there.

A bell rang and Rod leapt up. "I think we've been summoned!" He ran to a box nailed to a tree. He thrust his hand into the opening and pulled out a letter, then began to read.

Celebrities, good news! There are no more trials! Prepare yourselves for a jungle feast in celebration of reaching the final when the winner will be announced!

"Not more testicles," Cleo said.

"I'd eat an antelope's anus, I'm so hungry." Lenny rubbed his belly.

"Do you think there'll be any booze?" Rod sat down and tossed the letter in the fire.

"So, we're about to know who the winner is." Zach was thoughtful as he looked around at the other contestants. He ran his fingers through his hair and decided that it might be an idea to wash it - he wanted to look his best.

"Let's have a swim and smarten ourselves up." Cleo stood and sauntered past. Three pairs of eyes followed the contours of her rolling behind. The men grabbed their towels.

"Last in washes my socks!" shouted Lenny as he raced ahead, and in moments the jungle finalists were enjoying their last dip in the lagoon.

CHAPTER TEN

Jo was excited. It was the final day of *Jungle Survival* and very soon a winner would be announced. At last Zach would be free and she'd be able to speak to him.

She'd decided to do as Hattie suggested and had arranged for the large screen in her house to be set up in the front lounge. Guests were thrilled that there was to be a party that evening and the kitchen was preparing a buffet-style dinner with an Australian theme. As she walked around her hotel and checked the preparations, she tried to imagine how Zach was feeling. Would he be anxious or happy to be on his way home? Jo wondered if he would have to stay on for some coming-out-of-the-jungle publicity.

A porter hovered beside Jo and she began to direct him on how to arrange the seating in the lounge. Suddenly, the front door burst open and Hattie appeared, leading a group of animated people, who hung off her every word. She wore a battered old bush hat with corks dangling on lengths of string and they bobbed as she bounced into the hallway.

"And this is where young Zach, the Gypsy Chef, would play," she said and made a sweeping motion with her arm. "The little fella ran up and down this very corridor and I was always falling over his scooter." Her eyes misted over and she dabbed at the corners with a tissue.

Jo was stunned.

Hattie wore a khaki shirt and very tight shorts

with knee-high socks above her crusty old walking boots. She winked as she guided the group on. "And now we'll see the kitchens where his culinary career began. This way to culinary heaven, ladies and gentlemen."

Jo shook her head. Hattie was a law unto herself! No doubt the poor punters were paying way over the odds for the privilege of following in the Gypsy Chef's footsteps and Jo hoped and prayed that Hattie wasn't going to have them traipsing all over her house too.

The front door was wide open and an icy chill blasted in. As Jo hurried to close it, she noticed that the Christmas gnome was dancing. His flashing nose illuminated a large, hand-written sign.

Jungle Survival, the Gypsy Chef Tours - This Way!

* * *

Poppy sat in the office in Wardour Street and tried to focus on her job. She wasn't in the mood to compile Chef's folder and scowled as she laminated glossy photographs. With their usual efficiency, the Disney press office had sent far too many to include in the file, together with a zillion cuttings from his demos and lunch. There were glittering reports from the grand finale too.

Chef had called earlier and asked if she'd like to go out for a drink that evening. He apologised for his behaviour on their last night in Orlando and told Poppy that he didn't like to lose, either professionally or personally, and had decided to have another stab at asking Poppy out. After his foul mood at the airport,

Poppy had planned not to speak to Chef socially again. She wondered why some men considered themselves irresistible and thought that perhaps it was because she hadn't succumbed and he was driven to continue his pursuit. But as she gazed at the handsome face in the photographs, she wondered why she was resisting. Would it do any harm to have a drink and see how things felt on this side of the pond? Zach would be cosying up to Cleo as soon as they left the jungle and it wasn't difficult to see which way the jungle wind blew. Well, Cleo was welcome to him and Poppy had no doubt there would be another set of compromising photos making headlines in the coming weeks. *See how the glamour model dealt with that!*

Poppy returned to the file but looked up when her phone began to vibrate. It was a text from Chef. *Please, have a drink with me tonight?* She stared at the words and was about to tell him to get stuffed when a thought came into her mind. She was due in the pub to watch the final episode of *Jungle Survival.* Poppy frowned. She'd look such a loser if she was on her own. It would be far more creditable to have a handsome man in tow as Zach left the jungle - everyone would be eager to see Poppy's reaction but with Chef on her arm her dignity would remain intact.

The Cock & Bull at 8pm she texted, then sighed and continued her work.

* * *

Bob sat at the desk in his room and studied the email from Poppy. She'd forwarded clips from Chef's recent Epcot event and as Bob stared at the photographs from the grand finale, he shook his head. *Stupid boy!* Foam's and oils were so passé. The chef may have three Michelin stars but he wouldn't keep them unless he reinvented his menu and changed his signature dish. No wonder he'd come second to Pascal. Still, the publicity was brilliant and the Disney marketing machine had ensured that Chef was all over the media. Bob mentally calculated Chef's earnings for the event. The agency's twenty percent cut would soon be landing in Bob's bank account and he was confident that they would pick up a lucrative endorsement or two for Chef, stateside. All in all, it had been a successful trip and he made a note to reward Poppy with a bonus.

Bob scrolled through other emails. One of them made him pause. It was from a journalist friend who informed Bob that some interesting news, indirectly concerning one of his clients, was about to break in the press. Bob smiled when he read the name of the celebrity chef. It was very interesting indeed!

He stood and stretched then wandered out to the balcony. As he gazed at the view, Bob wondered if Anthony had been watching *Jungle Survival.* He'd tried not to think of his ex since he'd been in Australia and with Gary and Simon providing a welcome diversion, it hadn't been hard. But now, the reality of the homecoming drew close and Bob thought about his partner and the row which had led to their break-up. As the manager of a busy theatre, Anthony had always been a flirt. With hordes of actors passing over the boards, vying for attention when they were a long way from home, he was easily distracted. But his indiscretion with the lead actor of Pricilla Queen of the Desert, had been a flirt too far. It had shocked and upset Bob and he'd stormed out. Now however, considering Bob's own philandering on the other side of the world, he wondered if it really mattered in a long-term relationship. Did a moment of madness mean doom to the best thing that had ever happened to him; hadn't they vowed to be together through thick and thin? *Life was always so complicated!* But Bob had no time to think about Anthony; Zach would be leaving the jungle soon and with any luck, he'd be wearing a crown.

Bob walked back into the room and selected his favourite Ozwald Boateng suit from the wardrobe. It was burnt orange in colour and a lightweight fabric, perfect for the cameras and heat. He smoothed a tinted moisturiser over his skin and admired his reflection; the sun had deepened his tan and Bob thought that he looked extremely handsome. He dressed carefully then sat in the shade on a chair on the balcony, where the sun glittered across the water. Closing his eyes and letting his mind become calm, he uttered a few chants and prayed for a peaceful world and happiness for all humanity, including Anthony.

A phone rang in the bedroom. The coming-out show was planned for midday and with the time difference, would go out live on British screens at nine o'clock in the evening. The call was to instruct Bob to go down to the foyer where, alongside family and friends, he would be transported to the studio next to camp to wait for the celebrities. With a last lingering look in the mirror, he thanked his god for bringing them all safely to the end of Zach's days in the jungle and then stepped confidently out of his room.

* * *

"Bloody hell, these shorts are tight!" Hattie stuck her stomach out. A button popped and spun across the room. "It's like a furnace under this hat and the corks have played havoc with me hair." Hattie glared as she untangled strands of string and hair.

"Serve you right if you have to cut them out," Jo said and handed Hattie a pair of scissors.

Hattie pushed her away. "I thought you'd be a bit more grateful." She winced as Jo tugged hard on a cork. "I drummed up a crackin' bit of business and they're all coming back for the show tonight; tickets on the door will go like hot cakes."

"I didn't think you could get so many people in a vardo." Jo thought about the excited faces on Hattie's tour as they'd clapped eyes on the old gypsy caravan in the meadow.

"Like sardines." Hattie grabbed the hat and flung it to one side as Jo released the last curl. "Especially when I told them Zach was born in there; they were falling over themselves to get up the steps."

"But he was born in the hospital in Marland."

"And your point is?

"I wonder if Poppy has been watching the programme."

"Nah, she'll be hooked up with another handsome stud by now, a pretty girl like that."

"Such a shame, I really thought they'd get married."

"The world isn't perfect Jo, and your Zach is easily tempted."

"I still think he was set up over The Dolores Photos. That girl must have made a tidy sum."

"Aye, dream on." Hattie had shed her shirt and was stepping out of her wrinkled shorts. "By heck, it's good to get out of those passion killers." She peeled off her socks and threw them to one side. "Let's get glammed up tonight, we've got a full house and a lovely buffet to look forward to and I can't wait to celebrate Wonder Boy lifting that crown."

"You're right," Jo replied. "Let's go to town!"

"Catch yah later," Hattie said as she headed for the guest bathroom. "Bet you won't be as beautiful as me."

Jo heard the bathroom door slam and shook her head as she stared at the chaos around her. She picked up Hattie's discarded clothing and folded it neatly onto a chair. Tonight certainly was going to be a big night and Jo hoped and prayed that Zach would be crowned Jungle King and have his reputation restored in some way. She knew it was in the lap of the gods, but, deciding that she was going to enjoy every moment of her son's experience as it was shown to millions of viewers, she hurried to get ready.

CHAPTER ELEVEN

The Cock & Bull was packed and regulars flocked through the doors, eager to get a place in the pub where Zach was a local celebrity. Ben had erected a wide-screen on a wall across one end of the bar and customers were shoulder to shoulder as they crowded round. Poppy was jostled as she made her way through and people smiled as she approached, many remembering her as part of a couple when she was engaged to Zach.

Chef, dressed immaculately in designer jeans and a crisp white shirt, was already at the bar and waved when he saw Poppy. "I've made some space," he said from his elevated position on a stool and Poppy could see that they would have a clear view of the TV.

"Are you sure you want to watch this?" Poppy asked as she slid alongside.

"You bet," Chef replied and smiled.

Poppy could see that Chef was enjoying himself. He was probably convinced that Zach's celebrations with the glamour model were sure to end any lingering feelings that Poppy might have for her ex.

"I've got your favourite wine," Chef said and pointed to a bottle of Pinot Grigio. He lifted it from a bucket of ice and poured them both a large glass. "Cheers!"

Poppy sipped her drink. She looked around and saw Ben rushing to and fro and he winked when he saw Poppy. But despite Ben's reassuring smile, she was anxious. She wasn't sure if this was a good idea and wondered how she would feel when she saw Zach as the end of series celebrations splashed across the screen. He was sure to be wrapped around Cleo Petra and Poppy hoped that the sight of him with another would kill any sentiment she had left.

Heartened, Poppy felt Chef drape an arm around her shoulder and he leaned in and kissed her on the cheek. Turning her head to smile at him, she decided that tonight would put paid to the past and, finding his lips, Poppy returned the kiss.

Was a new chapter in her love-life about to begin?

* * *

Bob sat in a marquee with the contestant's friends and families and nodded when a waiter offered a buck's fizz. Why not? Today was going to be a celebration and Bob had to admit that he was looking forward to it.

The marquee had been erected as a screening room for the coming-out show and was festooned with balloons and huge arrangements of flowers. Bob hardly recognised the faces. Everyone was dressed to the nines and it was hard to place them in the same category as the fraught, casually-dressed group who had been trailing to and from their accommodation each day.

A blonde was weaving around the room. She wore a tight yellow dress and was taking advantage of the freely available booze. As she knocked back several glasses of wine, she roared with laughter and made a toast to "my rock-star hubby"; assuring the watching group that Rod Zephyr would be racing out of the jungle and into her arms, wearing the crown. Bob studied Mrs Zephyr carefully and decided that she resembled a banana, which was rather fitting, given the environment. A pretty brunette with a chirpy cockney accent held court with members of the press and declared that she was certain that 'her Lenny,' would soon be 'King Lenny' and she couldn't wait to be his queen. On the far side of the room, a huge muscled man, who'd not been there before, flexed his biceps and paced up and down and Bob wondered who the mysterious hulk was, but before he had time to make enquiries, a screen on one wall of the marquee flickered into life and Ava sprang into action.

"G'day!" she said, "or should I say, good evening to the folks in Britain!" The camera switched to the camp and Ava's voice-over explained that the celebrities had woken early to the news that they would soon be joining their loved ones. Zach, Lenny, Rod and Cleo could be seen sitting round a table groaning with food and drink. There was a cocktail bar in the background. The celebrities were chatting and appeared happy as they tucked into their first decent meal in weeks.

Bob watched Zach and thought that the chef looked wonderful. His thick black hair shone and he was toned, tanned and healthy. Weeks of abstinence had clearly done him good. Bob day-dreamed about the endorsements that would follow Zach's victory, perhaps something with a rugged outdoor theme, maybe men's cologne or a fitness clothing range? There would certainly be another TV series of the Gypsy Chef and more books, perhaps even an autobiography.

"Remember folks," Ava's voice burst through Bob's thoughts, "there are only a few minutes before we announce the results!"

Bob finished his drink and looked around for a bathroom. There was just enough time to powder his nose.

* * *

"Step this way!" Hattie stood by the front door and collected tickets from the assembled group on the driveway then ushered them from the hall and into the lounge. "Move along, there's plenty of room."

The sofas and chairs around the side of the room bulged with people and fully occupied seats formed lines in the middle. Jo's flat screen had been placed on a tall mantelpiece, giving everyone a good view. Christmas decorations twinkled alongside swags and garlands, creating a festive atmosphere and, as guests and hotel residents took their places, drinks were handed round.

"We need a swamp juice over there!" Hattie said to a waiter and pointed to an elderly man in a safari suit. "And a jungle juice for our friend in the corner." A middle-aged woman, wearing a costume consisting of chamois leather's tacked together with string, reached for a drink and waved.

"Do you think you've overdone it a bit?" Jo

looked anxiously at the bizarre collection of mid-lifers, who were dressed in a startling selection of fancy dress outfits. She spotted an elderly tiger on all fours in the bay window, alongside a wrinkled Tarzan and Jane; their skimpy costumes left little to the imagination.

"Are you joking?" Hattie was aghast. "Everyone's entered into the spirit of things, think of the bar sales! We should have a prize for the best-dressed."

Hattie wore a thick furry onesie, complete with ears and a tail.

"Who are you?" Jo asked as she stared at Hattie. Her friend had turned an odd shade of purple under all that fur.

"I'm the King of the Swingers," Hattie said and winked as she jiggled about. "Baloo the Bear, do you want to be my man-cub?" she began to sing. "Oh, oobee doo, I wanna be like you." Hattie grabbed a passing lion and swung him into a dance. "I wanna walk like you, talk like you..." She planted a kiss on his furry mane.

"I think I'll turn the heating off." Jo stared at Hattie as the lion attempted to twirl Baloo into a jive.

"Don't be long, the programme's about to start," Hattie called out over the lion's shoulder. She had broken out into a sweat and fanned her face with the end of his tail.

Jo went into the hall and fiddled about with the thermostat and, satisfied that the temperature would soon drop, took a drink from a passing waiter and returned to the lounge.

"Here he is!" Hattie shouted out and a cheer ricocheted as the final four celebrities appeared on the screen.

"Zach doesn't look very happy." Jo frowned and studied her son's face.

"He seems to be having a serious conversation." Hattie pushed the fur hood off her forehead and wiped her brow.

"Are you alright?" Jo asked. Hattie was a red as a raspberry and perspiring profusely, strands of hair stuck to her forehead.

"Just hot, I'll sit down for a second." She reached out to grab a chair and placed her padded behind on the seat. "Can you hear what's he's saying?" She wiped a furry paw across her face.

"I think they're all having some sort of confessional."

"Must be the drink. Grab us a glass of water, Jo."

* * *

In the Cock & Bull, all eyes were locked on the screen. There wasn't a sound in the room as they watched the jungle celebrities gather around a table, deep in conversation. The finalists had been drinking for the best part of an hour and, having pushed their empty plates to one side, seemed to have forgotten the cameras.

Lenny looked morose and told the group that he'd always wanted to go straight and regretted his years of crime. He admitted that it was a much happier way to live and was looking forward to getting married, having kids and bringing them up to lead a crime-free life. Rod twirled the beer in his glass and looked thoughtful as he studied the amber nectar. Without any warning, he suddenly announced that he was going to call time on his thirty-year marriage, for he'd fallen in love with a roadie called Rick and wanted to spend his remaining years rocking down the road to happiness, in a relationship that felt right. Lenny applauded and shook Rod's hand. Cleo sat forward and leant her chest on the table. As the camera zoomed in, she dabbed at tears on her hamster-like cheeks and admitted that she'd been having an affair for six months with a body-builder, who'd melted her heart. Cleo sobbed that he'd never told his fiancée about their relationship and she knew that he had to come clean; she'd be bereft if she couldn't spend the rest of her life nestling in his Amazonian embrace.

The crowd in the pub was on the edge of their seats as they stared at the screen. Ben leaned on the bar and wondered what the hell Zach was going to come out with. Poppy drained her glass and reached for a top-up, while Chef sat forward with a smile on his face.

"And so, my friend," Rod looked up and stared at Zach, "we've all been in the confessional, now what about you?"

Cleo sat in between Rod and Lenny. The men had placed their arms around her shoulders and the trio gazed searchingly at the Gypsy Chef.

"Oh, I don't know," Zach began, "I've made some stupid mistakes."

"Well, now's the time to tell us," Rod said. "Come clean, brother. I've just made sure my wife fleeces me for every penny I've ever earned." He shook his head.

"My reputation as a fraud is in tatters," Lenny replied.

"I'll have my face ripped off when I get home."

Cleo sobbed again as she thought of her lover's scorned fiancée.

"I wish I'd never gone up a mountain and got pissed," Zach whispered. He stared at his new friends. "I lost the only thing that I really want and now it's too late."

* * *

There was a silence in the marquee as the assembled crowd stared at the screen. The celebrity's confessions had stunned them all. Suddenly, a banana-like figure fell to the floor and began to scream and as Bob heard Rod's wife yell that she'd rip his balls off, Mac the Medic raced over to calm her down.

On screen, Ava was in the camp, and as the anxious celebrities greeted her she stated that she was going to announce the results.

Cleo was fourth.

The model leapt to her feet and began to squeal and, as she grabbed hold of Lenny, her breasts burst from her vest.

"Airbags!" Lenny said and hugged Cleo tightly.

Cleo adjusted her top and the camera zoomed in to catch her running across the bridge and into the arms of her body-builder, his engagement clearly off.

Ava then announced that Lenny was third.

He jumped up and thumped everyone on the back and, grabbing a handful of chicken drumsticks and a bottle of beer, lumbered over the suspension bridge. The paparazzi surged forward as Lenny flung his arms around his girlfriend.

"And now the runner up." Ava let the tension build.

Bob closed his eyes and began to chant. He transcended to the valleys of Nepal where a warm wind soothed his beating heart. When he opened his eyes he saw Rod running over the bridge and into the arms of Rick, who had magically appeared. Bob sighed and thanked his gods and remembered the email from his journalist friend.

The Delores Photos were about to be blown apart.

A premier league footballer had been tested positive for Rohypnol, a date rape drug, after compromising photos with a woman called Dolores had been shown on social media. The footballer, convinced that he had been drugged, was taking Dolores to court and the journalist felt sure that the Gypsy Chef had a case too. Bob smiled as he watched his client.

Zach was the newly crowned King of the Jungle.

* * *

Poppy was stunned. Had Zach really just said those words? She stared at the screen as she watched her ex-fiancé being crowned King of the Jungle and, despite his confession, wondered how on earth she could ever have him back after everything that he'd done. Clearly she'd been mistaken about Cleo and now realised that the programme was cleverly edited but nothing would ever edit The Dolores Photos. Poppy knew there no way forward in her relationship with Zach.

"Better have a butcher's at this," Ben said and reached under the bar. He pulled out the evening newspaper and thrust it under Poppy's nose.

Dolores Does It Again!

Poppy read the headline. The words didn't make any sense as she tried to digest the story of a footballer and a date-rape drug. She looked up at Ben and saw that he was smiling.

Chef, who'd scanned the headline too, slid off his stool. He shook his head in disgust and with a grunt, disappeared into the crowd.

"So, he didn't..." Poppy began.

"Looks that way," Ben replied.

"He must hate me for thinking he'd slept with Dolores deliberately."

"Well, I guess you and everyone else thought that."

"Oh, what have I done?"

* * *

"And the new King of the Jungle is, Zach, the Gypsy Chef!" Ava said.

The crowd gathered around the television in the hotel lounge exploded. The boomers in Boomerville leapt to their feet and began to hug each other. Someone put on a recording of the song, Jungle Rock, and everyone joined in the chorus, tails and paws swinging in time to the catchy rhythm.

Jo was jumping up and down too and tears poured down her face as she watched her son being led triumphantly across the suspension bridge to his throne, where all the other excited contestants crowded around him.

"Hattie! Hattie!" Jo yelled and turned to hug her friend.

But Hattie was slumped in her chair, her fur hood had twisted to one side, and Jo could see that her eyes were closed.

"Hattie?" Jo said and leaned down to touch her friend's face. "Are you alright?" Jo had a tremor in her voice and her hand shook as she reached out. Hattie's skin was clammy and she didn't appear to be breathing. In the background, the guests were singing: *For he's a jolly good fellow!*

"Hattie!" Jo screamed above the noise and began to tear at the Baloo costume, wrenching the furry chest apart. The guests had formed a conga and were dancing past Hattie's chair. Jo sank to her knees and cradled Hattie's head. "Don't die, you can't die," she whispered. "Please, please, stay with me!"

CHAPTER TWELVE

"It's a wonderful party!" Bob yelled above the noise. He was accompanying Zach around a function suite at the Willyumbah Palazzo where a band was playing and waiters circulated with trays of canapes and drinks.

"I've been trying to get hold of Mum," Zach shouted. "I can't wait to speak to her and Aunty Hattie and hear all their news."

Bob watched the crowds flocking around Zach and knew that the young man would make the most of the evening ahead. Women both young and old clamoured for the attention of the new King of the Jungle. Bob wondered when would be an appropriate moment to show Zach the Delores headlines. He decided that there was no immediate hurry, let the boy enjoy his victory; after all, Poppy might not want him back after all this time and she would have been watching Zach's steamy scenes in the jungle.

"I'm going to have a dance!" Zach laughed and waved at Bob before he was dragged away by Lenny, Cleo and Rod.

"Go and enjoy yourself, dear boy," Bob replied. The finalists had plunged Zach into the group of contestants, where he was carried shoulder high.

Bob glanced at his watch and thought about phoning Jo again. He too had been trying to get through to Marland, but Jo wasn't picking up her mobile. The receptionist at the hotel had told Bob that Jo was, 'currently unavailable', and he decided not to call again. Jo was probably having the party of all parties with Hattie and the two would be romping around the hotel and garden with a stampede of inebriated guests, as they celebrated the Gypsy Chef's victory. Bob felt sure that Jo would call him in the morning when all the fuss started to calm down.

Bob thought about home and wondered what Anthony was doing. He had hoped that there might have been a call or even a message. But his ex-partner was no doubt deep in the desert with Pricilla and not remorseful at all. Bob sighed.

"Hello there!"

Bob heard a familiar cry and turned to see his friends, Gary and Simon. "Come and dance," they both said and reached for Bob's hands to lead him to the dance floor.

"Perhaps I will," Bob replied and, straightening the collar on his suit, grabbed their hands and danced onto the floor beside them.

* * *

Poppy was in agony. She paced around the room, wondering how the hell she could have been so stupid!

Zach had pleaded with her to believe him.

He'd sworn that he hadn't slept with Dolores deliberately and couldn't remember a thing. But Poppy had raced to one conclusion and hadn't given

Zach a chance. Now, he would never forgive her! He would have had time to mull over their parting and would surely realise that if she hadn't believed him, then the trust that they had would always be broken.

Thank God she hadn't slept with Chef.

She'd been so very tempted. But Chef had shown his true colours when he'd read the Dolores headlines and hadn't stuck around to put up a fight. Perhaps Poppy's face had said it all and Chef had known there was no contest. She would never know.

Damn! Poppy closed her eyes and wished that she was on the other side of the world, celebrating Zach's success but she knew that her wishes were hopeless. Zach would be partying the night away and, with all the stunning starlets around him, he'd be spoilt for choice.

How could she have been so stupid!

* * *

Jo found it hard to remember what had happened. One moment she was celebrating Zach's success and the next she was in the back of an ambulance.

As she sat in the relatives' room at Westmarland Royal Hospital, Jo closed her eyes. Images of Hattie came flooding back and she felt hot tears burn down her cheeks.

Baloo the bear.

Jo smiled. She saw Hattie's ample body jiggling in the bear costume, her bottom swaying from side to side as she moved around the crowded room, making sure that everyone had their nibbles and drinks topped up and were having a good time.

What Jo would do to see Hattie jiggle and jive in

front of her now! The last she remembered was the flashing blue light of a response vehicle as it screeched to a halt on the drive. A doctor had rushed to Jo's side and gently moved her away.

"It's OK," he'd calmly said. "I'm with her now."

Jo had watched an ambulance arrive and stood back as Hattie was placed on a stretcher and carried out. Her deathly complexion was highlighted as they passed by the glowing nose on the Christmas gnome.

"I've bought you a cup of tea, dear." A nurse leaned in and touched Jo's arm. "Try and drink it, you've had a terrible shock. Is there anyone we can call for you?"

Jo thought about Zach.

He was thousands of miles away and would be partying. She must leave him alone for the time being. Bob too. It wasn't fair to spoil their celebrations. Perhaps she should call Jimmy in Barbados? But, at this stage, there was no point in worrying him as well.

"You can go and see your friend," the nurse said.

Jo's hand shook as she took the cup and saucer and tried to sip her tea.

"Would you like me to take you?"

"Yes... please." Jo put the drink on the table and stood. Her legs felt heavy and threatened to give way and as she moved one foot in front of the other, she took a deep breath. *She must be strong!*

The nurse led Jo through the corridors and tapped in a security code to allow them onto the ward. Jo felt like a zombie as she slowly moved forward into a curtained-off section.

Hattie lay on a bed. She was flat on her back and wires and monitors were everywhere.

Jo stepped quietly into the room and leaned in to

stroke Hattie's cheek. Drained of all colour, the skin was warm and for a fleeting moment Jo was filled with hope.

"Can I talk to her?"

"Yes, of course." The nurse pulled out a chair and Jo sat down.

"Does she know that I'm here?"

"No one knows." The nurse shook her head. "We just can't tell."

* * *

Bob was distraught. The phone call he'd received a few moments ago had sent him into a panic. His heart raced and he grabbed hold of the chair by his desk and eased himself down.

Dear God! Not Hattie! Hattie was larger than life and the rock that the family turned to. What on earth was he going to tell Zach? He knew that he had to get them both on a plane as soon as possible and must arrange flights. Why the hell did they have to be on the other side of the world when this terrible thing happened? Hattie was like a second mother to Zach and had been there from the moment he was born. The young chef spoke so lovingly of his godmother and the happy family times they had all shared.

Bob closed his eyes. He took a deep breath and tried to recall soothing chants that would help. A few minutes later he opened his eyes and stood up.

He was ready.

* * *

Zach lay on his bed and flicked through the celebrity

gossip on the internet where his face was plastered all over the press as the newly crowned King of the Jungle. He yawned. He was tired from all the fuss and endless interviews and would be pleased when the media attention died down and he could get on a plane and go home.

A curtain billowed and wind hurtled through an open window. It looked very stormy outside and Zach went to secure the panes. As he looked out, he could see that the sky was dark and menacing black clouds in the distance threatened rain.

There was a gentle knock on the door and Zach padded across the room to answer it.

"Dear boy," Bob said and stepped in. "We need to have a little chat."

"Have you managed to get hold of Mum?" Zach asked hopefully. "Her mobile seems to be off and the staff at the hotel say that she's still unavailable."

"Sit down." Bob took Zach's arm and guided him to a chair.

"What's wrong?" Zach suddenly felt a stab of fear as he looked into Bob's eyes.

Bob took a deep breath and felt a wave of calm wash over him. He reached out for Zach's hands.

"I'm arranging flights," Bob said. "We need to go home."

* * *

The unexpected storm swept through New South Wales. Rain lashed as thunder cracked the sky open and lightning bolts shot electrifying currents with a ferocity not seen in years. It was impossible to leave the hotel and, as the airport was closed, there was nothing that Bob and Zach could do but wait.

Bob had tried to speak to Jo but the phone connection was limited and he imagined that she was depending on her mobile and probably didn't have a signal.

Zach had packed all his belongings within moments of Bob's announcement and now stood by his cases staring out of the windows at the wild conditions beyond. Bob tried to encourage the chef to eat and ordered food from room service, but Zach had merely sipped water as he waited.

Twenty-four hours later the storm cleared and the two men leapt into the hotel's courtesy car and headed for the airport.

"There is some good news," Bob said as he checked that Zach had his passport. "Our flight from Dubai is now going straight to Manchester. The original tickets were for London so this will save some time." Bob thought of the effort the production company had made to get their newly crowned star home in his hour of need.

But the journey was unbearable.

Zach had never felt so far away from his family. There had been no messages from Jo other than to say that she hoped they had a good flight and Jimmy had called to say that he was heading in from the Caribbean and would meet Zach at home. As he stared out at endless cloud as the plane soared across the sky, Zach willed the journey to be over.

The stop-over in Dubai was seven hours and Bob asked Zach if he wanted to check into a hotel and get some rest but Zach refused to move from the departure lounge. He seemed scared to leave the airport, as if any deviation from their journey might cause a delay.

Eventually, they landed at Manchester.

The grey skies were welcoming and as Zach looked out at the cold sleet-like rain, beating against the windows, he longed to be with his family. They stood to leave the plane and Bob was thanking the cabin crew when an official came on board and asked them to step to one side. He told them that press had got hold of Zach's flight details and were waiting in the arrivals hall.

"Just smile and keep walking," Bob said as they went through customs; he knew that the last thing Zach wanted was to pause for photographs and interviews.

"I wish Mum was here," Zach whispered as they went through the green zone and headed for arrivals. Zach was pale and his face appeared strained and tired.

Bob took Zach's arm. He feared that the new King of the Jungle was about to break down. The press would have a field day. Manipulating both Zach and his own laden trolley, Bob instructed Zach to walk quickly. A car was waiting on the other side.

As they stepped into the arrivals hall, a cheer went up. Cameras flashed and a crowd surged forward.

"Tell us what it's like in the jungle, Zach!"

"Are you going to sue Delores?"

"Did you and Cleo get it on?"

Reporters fired questions and closed in and an eager crowd begged Zach for his autograph.

"Never mind all this bleedin' fuss!"

Zach was scrawling his name across a pad and as he handed the pen back to its owner, he looked up.

The mass of bystanders suddenly parted and an electric motor scooter burst forward and screeched to stop.

Strapped to the front of the scooter sat a tired old Christmas fairy.

"Wonder Boy!" A cry came from beneath a shabby old hat as corks swung haphazardly from the brim. "Never mind pretending that you're a celebrity, get yourself over here!" Hattie surged forward and stuck a walking boot out to fend off anyone unfortunate enough to be in her way.

Bob had gone white; he shook his head and wondered if he was seeing a ghost.

"Aunty Hattie..."

"Come on, give us a kiss!"

"But I thought..."

"Thought I was dead?" Hattie grinned and held out her arms. "Nah, there's years left in me yet." She wrapped Zach in a bear hug then pushed him away. "Now, where's your mam?" She spun the scooter round, scattering journalists in several directions.

Jo ran forward and Zach scooped her into his arms.

"Oh, Mum, it's so good to see you!" Zach cried as he held onto his mother. "And I can't believe Aunty Hattie is here."

"It was a virus, which went as quickly as it came." Jo looked over Zach's shoulder to Hattie. "The doctors say that she's a miracle and they've never seen anything like it before." Jo paused. "Thank goodness the antibiotics kicked in, because nothing was going to stop her from being here to welcome you home."

"Good to have you back!"

A voice called out from behind Hattie and Bob

looked up. Standing to one side of the crowd, Anthony clutched a huge bouquet of roses and looked sheepishly at Bob.

"Can you ever forgive me?"

"Oh, my dear!" Bob cried and fell into Anthony's arms. "We must never be parted again." The two men sobbed as they embraced.

As everyone said their hellos and greeted each other with tears of relief, officials swiftly ushered the reunited party towards their waiting cars.

"Oh, it's so good to be home," Zach said as he helped Hattie off her scooter and onto the back seat alongside Jo.

"There's just one more thing." Jo leaned forward and nodded to a figure that had appeared behind Zach.

Mystified, Zach turned in the direction that Jo had indicated. He stopped in his tracks.

Poppy stood beyond the kerb. A coat was draped over her shoulders and she was wearing the green sheath dress. She bit on her lip and looked anxiously at Zach. "Can you forgive me?" she asked.

'Oh, God," Zach cried and ran to sweep her into his arms.

"Oh God!" Bob repeated, "I don't think I can take anymore." And with a swoon, he grabbed hold of Anthony and dragged him into their car.

Jo patted a rug around Hattie's knees; it was in a tartan pattern with reindeers running across the fabric. She peered out through the window where the sun had come out and bright skies lay ahead. In the entrance hall under a sign announcing, *Arrivals*, a Christmas tree twinkled; the pretty lights bounced off the glistening pavement. Jo broke into a slab of

Marland Mint Cake and offered a piece to her friend.

"This'll put hairs on me chest." Hattie stroked the rug on her lap and sucked happily.

"Happy Christmas, Hattie," Jo said. "Aren't we lucky?"

The King of the Jungle and his soon to be Queen were still on the pavement and Hattie beamed as she watched Zach and Poppy embrace.

'By heck," Hattie whispered, and she reached for Jo's hand, 'we certainly are!"

Jungle Rock

ABOUT THE AUTHOR

CAROLINE JAMES

Caroline James was born in Cheshire and wanted to be a writer from an early age. She trained, however, in the catering trade and worked and travelled both at home and abroad. Caroline has owned and run many related businesses and cookery is a passion alongside her writing, combining the two with her love of the hospitality industry and romantic fiction. She writes fun, romantic fiction and is a member of the Romantic Novelist's Association. She has had numerous short stories published and as a food writer, writes regular columns for several magazines. Caroline can generally be found with her nose in a book and her hand in a box of chocolates and when not doing either, she likes to write, climb mountains and contemplate life.

www.carolinejamesauthor.co.uk
Twitter: @CarolineJames12
Facebook: Caroline James Author

If you enjoyed this book, you may also enjoy reading more from Caroline James

Coffee Tea the Gypsy & Me

Coffee Tea the Caribbean & Me

So, You Think You're A Celebrity… Chef?

Jungle Rock

* * *

Boomerville - publishing soon

Join the shenanigans at Boomerville, a retreat for discerning clients of a certain age. Find out if it is fun to be over fifty, single and serious about making the most of the rest of your life…

* * *

Printed in the USA
CPSIA information can be obtained
at www.ICGtesting.com
LVHW090554041224
798214LV00002B/242